William Berenger lives in Auckland, New Zealand.

For the *Fighting 10th* South Australian Battalion

William J Berenger

METAMORPHOSES

AUSTIN MACAULEY PUBLISHERS™

LONDON • CAMBRIDGE • NEW YORK • SHARJAH

A CIP catalogue record for this title is available from the British Library.

ISBN 9781398413238 (Paperback)
ISBN 9781398405141 (ePub e-book)

www.austinmacauley.com

First Published 2023
Austin Macauley Publishers Ltd®
1 Canada Square
Canary Wharf
London
E14 5AA

1. Fanny Durack

"For a woman to be exposed to public view as she is under the circumstances of surf bathing is utterly destructive of that modesty which is one of the pillars of our nationhood."

Archbishop Michael Kelly
Sydney Sun
14 August 1911

When Sarah Frances Durack was awarded the gold medal at the Stockholm Olympic Games in 1912, Fanny could not have imagined that her feat would be commemorated by lending her name to the statue of the Virgin; atop the steeple of Notre Dame de Brebières – Our Lady. Struck by a German artillery shell in 1915, the Virgin was left hanging precariously below right angles to the basilica.

Prostrate and semi-clothed, she salaciously reminded the soldiers of the 10th South Australian infantry battalion of their Olympic heroine winning the 100-metres freestyle in halcyon days, now four years long gone. Nervous anticipation superseded their fleeting carnal thoughts, which floated through the minds of many as they passed beneath Her for the front, which incidentally lay near the hitherto insignificant village of Pozières.

To the British, the Virgin was better known as the Lady of the Limp, as if Florence Nightingale could ever have imagined herself remembered as such a caricature. The Virgin's outstretched arms grasped the infant Christ. She resembled an inconsolably distressed mother about to fling her flailing child into the unknown night from a burning building, only to be dashed upon the unforgiving cobbles below.

If the lesser of two evils appeared to the Virgin to result in a similar *enfant perdu*, perhaps Christ would have preferred to die in the arms of His mother rather than be abandoned to the dark: alone. When suffering is intense, it won't be for long.

Fortuitously for the British, the steeple of Our Lady had offered an unobstructed panorama of their forward trench systems around Albert on the Somme. The Germans had correctly surmised that the belfry had been occupied by British spotters. Henceforth, even the sacrosanct Virgin and Child were unable to escape the attention of German artillery.

Acting Company Sergeant Major William Berenger had observed a feigned nonchalance in the Gallipoli veterans on the Western Front in the face of hardship and death. Moreover, Berenger became aware of a certain type of facetious black humour that acted as a temporary emotional panacea. He recognised from his own previous experiences that without treatment, this would eventually develop into a serious psychological condition.

Berenger noted a bawdy comment here or a guffaw there. In civilised circumstances in Adelaide before the war, such words would never have been uttered. Berenger observed a callous kind of laugh issue from their mouths, incongruous to their unsmiling eyes and otherwise grim expressions.

In reality, the horrors of the Western Front were indescribable. Seemingly, not a hint of emotion was shown by these men towards the lifeless, legless body of a young French soldier, who lay contorted amongst the rubble that had accumulated beneath Our Lady.

Covered in dust, this poor man's ravaged remains protruded rudely from fallen masonry and split timber. His comrades had not even the time, (nor probably the inclination as Berenger morbidly thought) to inter his body before leaving. Lifeless eyes stared directly up at the now prostrate Virgin and Child from a contorted dead face. A dusty forearm with a dead hand was displayed, grasping fingers and the glint of a gold wedding ring projected from the rubble as if macabrely waving *au revoir*.

***

Several of the men of the *Fighting 10th* (a sobriquet earned by the men from South Australia in blood and sacrifice for penetrating the furthest of any battalion on the Gallipoli peninsular) were thrown into the air by the indiscriminate explosions, which followed.

One of whom, *sans* right arm came to rest atop of the dead French soldier, who appeared to welcome him in a one-armed embrace. Berenger's morbidity disappeared.

He chided himself bitterly for not attending to the significance of the signs: the prostrate Virgin, the unburied *poilu*, the absence of civilians, the destroyed buildings, the drifting smoke, the faint smell of burnt flesh, and but for the presence of the South Australians – an eerie empty silence.

Berenger determinedly dashed atop the worn stone stairs of Our Lady overlooking the road. 3rd Australian Infantry Brigade superiors had issued assurances that the old pock-marked road would convey the South Australians uninterruptedly to Baupame and beyond, (but for the inconvenience of German-held positions around Pozières).

Through the ear-splitting explosions of the artillery barrage Berenger directed the *Fighting 10th* through the heavy basilica doors into the relative safety of Our Lady.

The bombardment finished as curtly as it had begun leaving many Australians groaning on the cobbles and several more, silent and dismembered. Berenger arranged three parties of three men to retrieve the wounded.

The Company Commander Major Meyer organised 1 and 2 platoons to secure the village under their platoon sergeants. He called the platoon commanders in no uncertain terms to parley with him as to why the village had not been secured first, before entering it: important lesson of the day 1.

Clutching his hanging left arm, within a tunic seeping with blood, Major Meyer kept issuing orders. However, due to severe blood loss and shock, he handed over temporary command to 25-year-old Captain Jack Hemple and stumbled into a side-chapel adorned with a crucified Christ. There, through blood-loss, he fainted on the stone floor. Subsequently, the side-chapel became the make-shift 10th battalion infirmary.

Berenger intended to remain with 3 platoon in the atrium of Our Lady to further establish a temporary company headquarters. He intended company HQ to relocate into the crypt to escape further shelling, once they had dealt with the consequences of being exposed to an enemy barrage in the open.

Battalion Headquarters was unwisely established at the crossing of the transept as it was central and there was more room in the nave when the pews were removed. Unwise, because the whole stone vault could have crashed down upon them if Our Lady was struck by a well-directed German artillery shell.

Depending upon who one was and what was their business, every entrance to the basilica adopted a different purpose. Entry for company matters in the atrium or battalion business in the transept was established through the main doors at the facade, which were thoroughly sandbagged.

The wounded were carried through a door in the axial chapel straight into the infirmary. If they died in the infirmary, the dead would be discretely removed for burial from the make-shift mortuary through a door in a side-chapel to the cemetery immediately beyond.

Battalion logistics, administration, signals, and medical personnel quickly established themselves and their fiefdoms in side-chapels, transept chapels, little niches along the aisles, and anything that could reasonably be considered available space including the altar. This was claimed by the battalion quartermaster's store momentarily before the Regimental Sergeant Major's disapproving scowl sent several storemen scurrying into the sacristy to reconsider their imprudent decision.

Exclusive rights to domains were claimed by creating enclosures with pews; marking lines with chalk obtained from beneath the topsoil in the fields surrounding Albert or imaginary lines, (which occasioned a disdainful glance followed by a gruff rebuke by the requisitioner if the unauthorised foot of a soldier happened to transgress).

The predominantly Protestant *Fighting 10th* transformed the Catholic religious centre of Albert into an efficient secular military establishment.

The Regimental Sergeant Major Warrant Officer First Class Mr Hoffman, (to which Berenger actually, rather than nominally deferred to) a deeply pious and exceptionally considered man, ramrod thin, steel-grey hair with deep furrows above his brows by his side-ways glance towards the quartermaster's men decided that adapting the sacred altar to a storeman's workbench was so indecorous that even in wartime special consideration should still be afforded to the religious feelings of the Catholic populace.

Revealing their inexperience of warfare on the Western Front before entering Albert, the Australians had not immediately realised why Our Lady was struck by the Germans. Considering Our Lady to be a target, which when destroyed would undermine the morale of the present Allied occupants of Albert; (and a tangible expression of the phrase *'Gott Mit Uns,'* which was indelibly engraved in relief into the belt buckle of every German soldier even if no longer as indelibly etched into their minds). The Australians incorrectly surmised that since She had been already hit, she was no longer a priority for the Germans.

Berenger concluded that if God existed, He had turned His back on His creation and did not care about what happened to either the Germans or the Australians. Berenger believed the symbol engraved in relief on the German belt buckle had come to be construed conversely as 'God has abandoned us'.

After the incessant slaughter since the outbreak of hostilities many of the German soldiers also begun to interpret it as such.

The nave of Our Lady had been selected as 10th battalion headquarters partially on the spurious grounds that a Church of God was always a welcome sanctuary to a believer and that the belfry had been struck inadvertently by a German artillery shell. But Berenger considered that God had left the Virgin and Child attached to the basilica misleading the soldiers that He actually cared.

Berenger calculated that he would be more protected from shrapnel by the heavy stone masonry surrounding him as he stood atop the stairs of Our Lady unless an enemy shell exploded directly to his front. When a corporal from the first rescue party pointed to a deep gash across Berenger's forehead finishing above his left eye from which his skull was exposed, Berenger merely stared back blankly at him.

The rescue parties darted out to retrieve the wounded and then the dead. When blood trickled into Berenger's eyes he realised his injury was worse than he had originally thought. The pain of the wound began to overtake him as the adrenalin disappeared. Although he had all but recovered from the physical scars of the Gallipoli Campaign, Berenger had never managed to recover from the intrusive memories that plagued his sleep. Emotional numbness and in this instance an overwhelming sense of guilt over the death of Private Wiremu Tamehana of the Auckland Infantry Regiment.

***

Modern artillery had evolved during the Industrial Revolution with ever more devastating effects. The

13

cataclysmic destruction delivered by the German 'five nines' could not be matched by British artillery until the six-inch howitzer was introduced onto the battlefield in late 1915. At least then the protagonists of the Triple Alliance and Triple Entente could equitably and equanimously slaughter each other.

Modernism had promised the benefits of a more rational, industrial and progressive society. Western society had indeed technologically progressed, but the heart of humanity had remained the same: many self-interested, indifferent or numbed to the suffering of the individuals, bearing its unintended burden. For the British army the tangible nadir of this realisation was the first day of the infantry Battle of the Somme – the 1st July 1916; the day the British Empire suffered the detriment of 57 470 casualties.

Nevertheless, the intellectual nadir was the realisation that the industrialisation of Western society for all of its propitious benefits had merely succeeded in creating evermore ingenious ways to inflict human suffering but on an industrial scale: progress.

***

Berenger, blood now streaming down his creased face, tottered, turned and entered the basilica. He steadied himself against one of the wooden pews. A moment's pause to reflect. Berenger's eyes adjusted to the dim *sfumato* of coloured light permeating those stained-glass windows, which had not yet been broken in the artillery barrage. Shards of light pierced the suffocating atmosphere to reveal figures of soldiers carrying in the wounded.

Cries diminished to muffled groans as the mortally wounded were carried as awkwardly as Christ deposed into the make-shift infirmary beyond the transept of Our Lady.

Ears still painfully ringing from the barrage of explosions outside Berenger discerned a calm stillness in the air, interrupted only by the faint smell of incense permeated by cordite. Although not spiritual himself, he sensed a deep spirituality within the basilica by a heightening of his residual senses: the sickly-sweet taste of his blood from that which had not coagulated on his face; the touch of the worn back crest of the pew, which his hand now unsteadily grasped giving warm comfort to many before him.

Berenger bent his head and looked down at the worn floor. A light-headed sense overcame him and he dropped to one knee to allow the dizziness to dispel. At that moment, a slender pale arm placed itself over his shoulder.

"May I help you, sir?" enquired an ethereal feminine voice in the Australian form of addressing a Warrant Officer Second Class.

"You speak English," Berenger replied weakly, still on one knee now looking at the hem of a nun's habit and in particular the pretty bare feet with almost translucent skin protruding from beneath.

Berenger pursed his lips and a scowl spread upon his face to repress a stirring, which began to emerge in his mind. His thoughts turned to Juliana, who waited for him heavily pregnant in Adelaide. Slowly and tentatively, he rose to his feet, breathing deliberately and steadily to oxygenate his blood. Regaining his senses, the dizziness dissipated.

Drawing himself to attention, Berenger formally introduced himself.

"Acting Company Sergeant Major William Berenger, 10th South Australian Infantry Battalion. How may I be of assistance?"

A kindly young female face smiled back.

"How may *I* be of assistance, sir?"

Her eyebrows expressing genuine concern above deep brown eyes. Eyes so dark brown as to be barely discernible in the half-light from dark dilated pupils. Her skin, translucent white with a wisp of dark brown hair ever so slightly protruding from her starched white coif.

All of about 20 years old, her firm grip had moved to Berenger's forearm to steady him. Berenger looked at her, white fingers pressing into his flesh through the coarse fabric of his tunic. The grip was sturdy but Berenger noticed that the tips of her fingernails, short and clean, did not reveal the pressure that her hand was exerting to keep him upright.

"Strange," he thought.

He then looked directly into her dark brown empathetic eyes positioned only about two inches lower and less than a foot away from his. A cynical smile appeared on the left-hand side of Berenger's face, which was correctly interpreted as: "I am fine now. Please remove your hand."

At the time, when the hand was removed from his forearm Berenger buckled at the knees and collapsed unceremoniously backwards, striking the back of his head upon the stone floor in doing so.

Now bleeding from both the back and the front of his skull, the thud on the floor caused him to regain consciousness yet again. Despite the seriousness of his wound to his forehead, Berenger had the presence of mind to feel extremely embarrassed.

The young woman crouched next to him, regained his forearm and said in a gentle voice, "Stubbornness will only make matters worse for you, sir. Your rank does not count in here. My name is Edith. Edith de la Croix. Please allow me to assist you."

"Yes…Yes of course," Berenger maffled an unconvincing response.

"Please call me, William. But Mr Berenger will do, in front of the troops."

Edith assisted William to his feet. He was impressed with her physical strength as much as her Elysian presence. Originally intending to make his way to the infirmary, Edith led William into the mortuary because it was closer.

Unfortunately, the mortuary was already beginning to fill with the battered bodies of what were once young South Australians. This included Berenger's company commander, who had been shifted from the infirmary where amongst the already deceased, he had quietly and stoically passed away.

Although at first, he did not show it, Berenger was overcome with grief at seeing his friend lying unceremoniously dead on the dank stone floor. Finally, he slumped onto two pews pushed together to make an uncomfortable bed. He felt Edith's gentle hands lift his head and place a rolled blanket under his neck.

Despite the injuries to his face and back of his skull, to attempt to remain conscious Berenger concentrated on her crucifix, which dangled mesmerizingly before his eyes. Edith carefully undid the top button of his tunic to allow him to breathe more comfortably. Refocusing on two peach-shaped orbs protruding from beneath her habit, and using approximately zero percent of his prodigious powers of deduction, Berenger determined that beneath her simple threadbare, off-white gown, Edith was naked.

Berenger closed his eyes. In effect to stimulate his imagination but ultimately he felt himself drifting off. He vaguely heard muffled voices say, "He's gone, Puck. C'mon mate, we got work to do."

Then Berenger felt a blanket being draped over his whole body as he lay supine on his makeshift bed and then nothing. Strange dreams entered his mind. Edith was removing his boots, bathing his head wounds and talking gently to him.

"Stay awake. Stay with us, sir." Berenger heard a soothing voice.

"Just let me rest my eyes." Berenger thought but did not say.

Eyes closed, he felt Edith gently peel back the cover from over his head; gently caress his blood-congealed hair. Her breath was close now. Berenger imagined a forbidden kiss: a sweet tear dropping from Edith's dark brown eyes onto his face and trickling into the corner of his mouth. He savoured the salty droplet. Berenger mentally forced his eyes to gradually open to gaze upon this heavenly angel.

"Puck! What in the Devil's name are you doing?" Berenger rasped at the ugly face of the company commander's batman, which had inadvertently dripped mucus from his snub nose into his Sergeant Major's mouth, as he peered intently at him trying to determine whether he was still alive or dead.

"I'm sorry, sir. We thought you was dead!" exclaimed Puck, taken aback.

A wave of halitosis entered Berenger's nose, instantaneously bringing him back to his senses.

"Well, I'm not bloody dead, I am?" Berenger whispered angrily.

Berenger's reserve and composure returning, he said, "You're a good boy, Puck. Now on your way. You've got work to do."

2. The Craven

"When Aristodemus returned to Lacedaemon, reproach and disgrace awaited him; disgrace, inasmuch as no Spartan would give him a light to kindle his fire, or so much as to address a word to him; and reproach, since all spoke of him as 'the craven.' However, he wiped away all his shame afterwards at the battle of Plataea."

Herodotus
Histories 7.231

The sun slipped below the South Australian horizon, leaving the cerulean sea gently lapping at the shore as had been solemnly observed by the Kaurna people for more than 40 000 years.

William sat in that uncomfortably straight-backed formal way that aspiring gentlemen, who are not entirely familiar with the affairs of women, sit. The chesterfield had been cleverly relocated to the narrow landing outside between the railing and the facade on the veranda of William's little country cottage for Juliana to enjoy the last rays of the setting sun with him.

'Cleverly relocated' so when Juliana had to squeeze by to sit down, her knee (encased in a slightly out-of-fashion, full length, three-gored, high collared, high buttoned, lace-trimmed calico dress complete with cream-coloured gloves and a matching cream-coloured, home-made Gainsborough hat) casually brushed against William's father's somewhat over-sized pinstripe black barrister's trousers, (which encased William's knee) causing William to sit even more uncomfortably, now fully erect.

"More iced tea, Mr Berenger?" Miss Fischer, housekeeper and matronly spinster enquired, simultaneously filling William's elaborately decorated teacup.

"Yes, thank you Miss Fischer," William responded red-faced but politely.

"You have hardly touched yours at all, Miss Kruger," Miss Fischer said smiling.

The muscles of her left cheek drawing her mouth crookedly but affectionately towards the left side of her face.

"But I have had such a wonderful time, Miss Fischer. William, I mean Mr Berenger and I have had such a wonderful conversation."

A large male kangaroo now silhouetted upon the hill, disinterested up until that point in time raised his head and stared blankly at Juliana, causing her to blush. The Kangaroo disconcertedly hopped over the crest of the hill to find more suitable pastures.

Wilhelm Berenger, barrister-at-law, William's father had invested in a modest cottage for William, as much to keep him out of the public eye as for his previous military service to Australia.

Although relieved that his son had survived Gallipoli, William's account of his injury to his back did not withstand the scrutiny of his father's incisive cross-examination. From the moment William had returned to Adelaide, where Juliana had met him at the port there were too many whispers of pusillanimity.

"Injured his back he said," was cruelly whispered in disbelief within earshot, with the emphasis on the word, 'back'.

"I say you're a coward," was anonymously shouted at William from an upstairs window as he limped past in a now loose-fitting uniform. The accuser quickly withdrew from the window when Juliana responded with the steely-eyed glare inherited from her Boer mother.

William began to understand their anguish but this did not alleviate his shame nevertheless. He felt their anger was directed at him because he had returned from Gallipoli, whereas many of the sons of South Australia, whose names had been published in the *Advertiser* had not.

The anxiety of not knowing the fate of a loved one was as distressing as the grief felt upon reading the name of one who had been killed. Or the covered-mouth grasp of concern for one, whose wounds were euphemistically described in the Adelaide *Advertiser* as 'light'. How could William expect anyone to understand a Turkish hand-grenade when the ANZACs had been filling old jam-tins with explosives?

For the people of Adelaide, the pending arrival of the newspaper began to contagiously intensify feelings of anxiety followed by the dread of reading it. Tears of relief or inconsolable grief again and again indelibly permeated a street, a family, a friend or a fiancée, who recognised a name.

The time, the place, the size of the letters in the newspaper, the place where the ink did not completely fill in the letter 'K' in the words, 'Killed in Action' became forever emblazoned on their minds.

Many male members of families, who lost loved ones managed to retain their stoic reserve in public, only to retire to a private room to weep tears of sorrow evermore bitterly. William understood it was not only armies but whole societies that suffered in war.

A simple wooden off-white cottage in the Victorian style with a lattice veranda, whose overgrown gardens were certainly in need of care and attention became William's home. The cottage and fireplace were structurally sound and the rooms, although small were tidy and comfortable. William's father had sent his housekeeper, Miss Fischer to look after William whilst he recuperated from his injuries.

Juliana returned to her lodgings in town. William sat despondently on the veranda surveying his overgrown domain. Miss Fischer cooked greasy bloaters for dinner, which he declined to eat. William remained sitting catatonically silent in the wicker chair on the veranda until the stars twinkled and the chill air brought Miss Fischer outside with a cup of hot cocoa and escorted him to his room; where he lay listlessly on his bed, sadly looking at the stars through an open uncurtained window. He reflected upon his experiences at Gallipoli where unfamiliar stars bore witness to history.

This process lasted several days. Several days turned into several weeks, with no visitors but Juliana. William waited diligently for her to sit with him on the veranda and watch the galahs land on the fence separating the property from the road.

He hardly spoke and rarely made eye contact with her. But Juliana, wise beyond her years talked to him about her childhood in South Africa.

Although William did not respond, Juliana could see that buried in his thoughts, he appreciated the therapeutic nature of the conversation.

Miss Fischer had scrupulously tidied the inside of the house; refreshed with pleasantly fragrant flowers every Sunday morning upon William's bedside table. William, Juliana, and Miss Fischer would then attend Sunday Lutheran service, where the minister extolled highly exaggerated tales of the martial infallibilities of South Australian soldiers to the congregation.

After several weeks of having been ignored by almost everyone at the service including the minister, William said to Miss Fischer that he no longer wanted to attend.

At precisely 9:00 am every Monday, Miss Fischer would take William into town to attend with Dr Frick, who inspected the progress of his physical injuries. Dr Frick's medical practice had recently become very busy treating returned servicemen; some of whom had completely lost any sort of military discipline and motivation. They leaned against the wall on the footpath outside, hands in pockets, shoulders slumped, dishevelled in appearance and downcast in demeanour.

So much so, that Dr Frick's assistant had observed that as ladies and children approached, they would cross the road before encountering the queue of miserable returned servicemen; increase their pace whilst passing parallel to them only to recross the road further down the street and regain their regular gait. Whilst the children would point and stare, the ladies often pretended to be fascinated by some article displayed in a shop window or intentionally stare straight ahead whilst they made haste to pass by.

This did not go unnoticed by William. But as he was at this point struggling to maintain his discipline, he felt it would be hypocritical to censure others for behaviours he knew he demonstrated himself. William returned home with Miss Fischer and sat sombrely by himself in his wicker chair, lost in his thoughts.

Feeling empathetic for the sense of embarrassment caused to these broken men, Dr Frick's assistant opened the medical practice half an hour early to allow them to assemble in the foyer; smoking sullenly or morosely lolling about out of sight of the public. The offer of hot tea was never declined, despite being served with neither milk nor sugar. A few kind words from Dr Frick's assistant often elicited a witty retort to reveal that one or two of them had mostly but not entirely lost their sense of humour.

William's mind often returned to Gallipoli to the New Zealand soldier, Wiremu Tamehana. William had thought about Wiremu's sacrifice over and over and over again; disconcertingly, even in his dreams.

At Gallipoli, Wiremu and William had crawled back through No Man's Land between the Turkish and the New Zealand trenches. By the starlight William could even see the sandbags above the New Zealand parapet. They were so very palpably close, but Wiremu believed they had been spotted. So, he stood up to attract Turkish rifle fire upon himself to enable the others to scramble safely into the New Zealand trench. Wiremu calculated the New Zealanders would recognise the *haka* and not fire at the Australians caught out in No Man's Land.

"Why did Wiremu do that?" William mumbled to himself over and over again.

He was so close, so very close. Wiremu could have survived. If only he hadn't stood up. The thought went around William's mind many times and every time he came to the same irrational conclusion: if it hadn't been for him, Wiremu could have made it.

***

Miss Fischer would not allow William to remain in bed after 7:00 a.m. Breakfast was served at precisely 7:30, which Miss Fischer would watch William eat; with arms folded and lips pursed if necessary.

William would always be required to be presentable in the mornings with a mild rebuke if he was not. After which he was allowed to sit on the veranda and watch the galahs land on the fence. At least their bickering and screeching at each other in anticipation of food brought some animation to William's face even if not entirely positive until one particularly noisy mid-morning William had had enough and stood up, shaking his fist and yelled, "For Christ's sake, shut up!"

At which time all but one flew away in a big arc to which William knew they would soon return. The one which stolidly remained was so old, he had hardly a pink feather or a grey feather to his name. He always sat on the outside of the group with one paltry plume sticking out of his head like an antenna.

"You look pathetic. Look at you. What bloody use are you to anybody, anyway! Piss off!" Berenger vitriolically cursed the dumb bird.

William began to laugh somewhat hysterically then cry a little, bringing Miss Fischer hurrying to the veranda. Miss Fischer called on Juliana, who was preparing legal files at the practice of Wilhelm Berenger, Barrister-at-Law. Juliana was permitted a half-day off and sat talking with William about her home in South Africa until the stars came out. The chill air brought Miss Fischer to the veranda again to escort Juliana home and usher William to bed, where he read Oblomov's Dream by candlelight with cocoa.

William began to believe that Oblomov suffered from *ennui*. Although probably caused by outside influences, ultimately the cause of Oblomov's failure to get out of bed was his own. Deciding that Oblomov was as superfluous as Pushkin's Eugene Onegin, Lermontov's Pechorin, and Tolstoy's Pierre Bezukhov all rolled into one, William became determined not to manifest the pejorative characteristics of any of them.

The next morning William rose early, made Miss Fischer breakfast and talked with her about the overgrown garden. He asked Miss Fischer about the kind of flowers she would like to see next spring and set about the task of tidying up outside.

Miss Fischer suggested that William design something in the Gardenesque style with winding paths and urns placed aesthetically in the curves. William walked to the fence and cast a critical eye back at the cottage for the first time since he had lived there.

He decided on the geometric Victorian style but he thought he should soften the strict linearity of his home by fixing a wooden lattice to an exterior wall, which would attract the evening sun. This would permit creepers to softly envelop the sunny-side of the cottage with green leaves interspersed with white inflorescences. William then planted saplings meticulously spaced to minimise cracking in the pavement when mature. Where hopefully, Juliana could paint or read and even more hopefully where their as yet, unconceived children could play in the shade.

One morning, whilst digging in his garden William paused, stood up and scratched his head. The Pattern 08 Entrenching Tool used at Gallipoli was equipped with a caste-steel pick and a shovel with a bevelled blade fixed at 90 degrees to the wooden handle.

William considered that it wasn't very good for digging downwards but more useful for a kind of scraping motion or picking at the ground to remove rocks. Furthermore, the shape of the entrenching tool did not lend itself to be carried around conveniently, nor did the handle lend itself to the optimum force required to fill the blade.

William preferred a straight blade in line with the shaft, similar but a little shorter to the one he was presently using. He thought about all kinds of shovels he had used in the past including a coal shovel with a wide blade but decided upon a wide blade of strengthened steel, which came more to a point rather than a flat edge.

"Hmmm, how could I simultaneously carry my rifle and my entrenching tool into battle?" he mumbled to himself.

Further ideas began to germinate in William's mind: "An adjustable sling!" he exclaimed to himself out loud in a 'Eureka' moment.

William wiped the sweat from his brow, walked briskly to the veranda and removed his boots. He made his way into the kitchen, located some writing paper and a pencil, sat down at the kitchen table and began to design a new entrenching tool.

Presently, he went back outside to retrieve his spade just as the minister of the local Lutheran church happened to call. He had noted that William had avoided attending Sunday services (and thereby no longer donated into the plate). After some fawning and disingenuous counselling to which, William said nothing but leaned on his spade in his garden.

William decided the minister was an unwelcome guest. The old featherless galah perched on the fence, listening intently to the minister's disingenuous ramblings, cocked his head to one side and squawked, "Piss off!"

3. Nil Desperandum

"We don't rise to the level of our expectations, we fall to the level of our training."

Archilochus (c.680-c.645 BC)

The adjutant of the 10th South Australian Battalion was an old friend and a welcome guest. William welcomed him in for tea. By the serious expression on Captain Wolff's face and dour demeanour of his body language, William discerned Captain Wolff had not merely intended to take refreshment.

"Sergeant Berenger," he said, before pausing to consider.

William frowned at the reference to rank. He was no longer a sergeant.

"Next year, South Australia will be required to raise another battalion."

Silence. Captain Wolff, despite concealing a significant part of his face behind his hand and his teacup was scrutinised surreptitiously by William. He appeared to gaze nonchalantly through the kitchen window, which overlooked the lilac blooms smiling in the garden. But in reality, he studied Captain Wolff's face in the reflection of the window. William had predicted the next question before Captain Wolff had formulated the words in his mind to ask it. He knew that Captain Wolff would ask him to re-join the colours.

William did not want to re-join the army. He believed he had served Australia and he had given Australia everything. He had returned from Gallipoli both physically and mentally scarred. Being called a coward upon his return because he had injuries to his back had psychologically cut him more deeply than the injuries themselves. He was resentful because those cruel comments revealed to him that even if he was willing to return to service, he was not ready.

William took a little sip of tea through pursed lips. He noticed that as he precisely held the tiny teacup between his thumb and forefinger, his little finger had inadvertently begun to protrude at a pretentious angle. The image immediately caused a wince, an imperceptible tick, not discerned by Captain Wolff.

William's eye withdrew from the tip of his little finger and traced down the outside edge of his hand to rest upon the blue veins on his right wrist; through which, blood continuously flowed back to his heart. Involuntarily, his heart beat causing bright red blood to pump quietly back into his hand; thereby, ensuring at least for another heartbeat, William's earthly existence.

The image caused William to pause, to narrow his eyes, and focus on his veins as they disappeared into his forearm. William, not always conscious of his own sentience, upon this momentary deliberation of his existence knew that he had not given everything to Australia.

He pondered whether at the point of his death, he would be permitted to review his life. William hoped he could say before he died that every second, of every minute, of every hour, of every day he gave it everything because at the point of his death, there was nothing left to give. He hoped that he could say that he had faced adversity bravely, accepted victory with humility and defeat with grace. He hoped that he would be permitted to look into his heart at the moment of his death and discover that this was true.

William balanced these considerations with his future with Juliana and with children, who had not yet come into, (and pending his decision, may never come into) existence. He knew he had the freedom of choice to remain in South Australia or return to the colours.

Discharged from the army as an invalid, Captain Wolff would accept his decision to remain in Australia as a considered but not a cowardly decision. But ultimately, William knew that if he decided against re-joining the colours, his hopes upon his deathbed would be disappointed.

William determined that he could not in all conscience say that he had given Australia everything if he declined Captain Wolff's offer. That Australia was at war was not of his making. William felt he was an insignificant cog in history but realised that he was not a helpless one. He decided to accept Captain Wolff's proposition.

Although he resignedly came to his conclusion, William was determined to say, 'Yes' in a considered and non-emotive manner. Not a 'Yes' that meant 'No'; not a 'Yes' that meant 'Maybe', neither enthusiastic nor reluctant, he would pause momentarily to consider and say without drama or dogma, 'Yes'.

Either way, William believed there was talk of conscription and despite his previous recent service and subsequent injuries, where a refusal could be declined with honour, he still felt had little choice.

"Sergeant Berenger," enquired the adjutant in a slightly higher tone.

Berenger straightened his back.

"We require your services as a non-commissioned officer in the 43rd Battalion, which will be raised in South Australia next year."

Berenger paused. Placed his teacup carefully on the table. Inhaled and without saying "Yes" or "No" decided to answer in the ambiguous manner of a non-commissioned officer with, "Sir."

"We will be glad to have you back, Staff Sergeant." Captain Wolff smiled and held out his hand to shake.

Newly promoted Staff Sergeant Berenger's cynical smile, developed in the Boer War and honed in training before the Gallipoli landings evolved further with an expectoration at the end of it, which sounded a bit like, 'ha!'

Captain Wolff continued, "The Battalion will be raised by March 1916. You have been nominated as a Quartermaster Sergeant. The Battalion Commander is Lieutenant Colonel G. Your Company Commander is Major Meyer."

***

Morphettville Racecourse was a hive of preliminary 43rd Battalion activity with the erection of bell-shaped tents into an orderly tent city. When Berenger arrived, he avoided the immediate introduction to his company commander and conducted a reconnaissance of the race-course pavilion;

destined for the Regimental Quartermaster's store. Upon entry, he discovered it was empty.

A broom head followed by its handle attached to the hands of a skinny 18-year-old boy in neat civilian attire produced itself at the far end of the pavilion from Berenger. A second and a third broom-handling teenager followed, each looking younger and skinnier than his predecessor. They did not look up but energetically began to sweep the concrete floor in unison towards Berenger, who stood at the near end of the empty pavilion.

"Good morning, men," Berenger bellowed.

The sweeping stopped abruptly and the boys stood to attention seeing a veteran in uniform, holding their brooms correctly in their right shoulders as if they were rifles.

Staff Sergeant Berenger marched directly towards the adolescents, who braced themselves ever higher as he approached. Crashing his right foot onto the concrete floor, eight paces in front of the right-hand man of the three, coming immediately to attention.

"Stand at...ease!" he growled.

Berenger gave the drill command, in a booming voice. Followed by a pause, he looked directly into the earnest faces of these young charges. Correctly, the boys' eyes were at 45 degrees above the parallel. Moreover, their eyes did not move.

A minute of silence, whilst Berenger assessed the character of these boys.

"Stand still," he growled again: this time in a whisper.

They had not moved. Berenger reflected upon his character at that age: ill-disciplined, motivated by his inward concerns rather than any patriotic fervour for his country and certainly not eager to serve South Australia by fighting in

South Africa. He was quietly proud of the boys and simultaneously felt the pangs of sadness and grief as if within a year he knew that the lives of all three of these young fellows could be extinguished.

In a more avuncular fashion, he said, "Men. Stand…easy. My name is Staff Sergeant Berenger."

"Marker!" Berenger issued the drill command.

The first boy, on the right-hand side of the trio came to attention and called out, "Staff!"

"Name?"

"Staff, Watts! Staff."

"Good! Next."

As the first boy adopted the position of 'Stand-at-Ease', the second boy came to the position of 'Shun'.

"Staff, I'm Watts too! Staff."

"Good! Next."

Berenger stood sternly at attention, staring straight at the third and smallest boy, who hesitatingly came to attention.

"Staff, Lachlan! Staff," the boy said nervously, (which elicited a snigger from the boy standing next to him).

"Shuddup!" Berenger boomed.

"Surname only. There's a good man," Berenger resumed his avuncular tone.

The boy obviously proud of his new appellation, 'man', more confidently stated, "Staff, Watts, Staff" in a quiet voice.

The cynical smile appeared momentarily, disappeared and returned as a genuine smile towards these young lads.

"Stand easy, men," he continued in a friendly and assured fashion.

The straight faces of these young men all simultaneously turned to enthusiastic smiles as Berenger approached and shook each of them by the hand and said, "Good morning, Private Watts," from eldest to youngest; after which the eldest, Albert said, "We're not proper privates yet, staff. We're still cadets."

"I stand corrected, Cadet Private Watts…the elder," Berenger added, to distinguish him from Watts, the middle, and Watts, the younger.

"Staff, I'm Cadet Sergeant Major Watts, staff," said the eldest Watts, deferentially.

"Edward and I are twins and this is our younger brother, Lachlan. We are all 18."

Lachlan Watts went red and lowered his eyes. Berenger, observing Lachlan Watts' embarrassment, frowned and momentarily considered the improbability of them all being 18.

Postulating the confusion, which would arise when addressing the Watts' boys only by their last names, Berenger held his thumb under his chin and his forefinger on his lips.

"I will address you by your cadet rank followed by your surnames until you have officially joined 43 Battalion. At that point, I will address you by the last digits of your regimental number followed by your surname. Are there any questions?" Berenger added.

All three came to attention, and said, "Staff, no, staff."

"Carry on," Berenger said softly.

The boys carried on sweeping, ever more vigorously in the knowledge that should they be accepted into 43 Battalion and given regular rank.

At that moment, through a sliding entered a dandily dressed, middle-aged man in a tweed suit with a hint of chalk dust on his pudgy fingers.

"Schoolmaster," Berenger thought.

"Good morning, sir," the man in tweed said, extending his hand.

"Sir, 'good morning staff,' sir," Berenger corrected, then saluted.

The gentleman in tweed abruptly came to attention and conducted an unusual salute with his pudgy fingers extending from his puffy palms in naval fashion but touching his right ear rather than correctly at his right eye.

"Sir, you needn't salute me. I am not an officer and you are not wearing a headdress, sir."

"Oh. Oh. I'm dreadfully sorry, please accept my apologies, sergeant," to which Berenger as not yet having sewn his new rank onto his tunic, realised the gentleman logically addressed him by his previous rank did not explode in a tirade of expletives.

Berenger came to his senses and replied more appropriately, "Please let me apologise for my over-formality. My name is William Berenger. I am the Company Quartermaster for Major Meyer's Company, 43 Battalion."

"William! I am so pleased to meet you. I am Mr Horace A. Pickle, Latin Master at Jesus-on-the-Torrens Charitable Public School for Boys, where the Watts' boys have served in the cadets these past four years."

Berenger tried to suppress a frown when Mr Pickle had referred to him informally as 'William' but referred to himself formally as Mr Pickle.

Mr Pickle excitedly added, "I am the new Regimental Quartermaster."

Berenger summoned all his discipline not to slump his shoulders upon hearing that revelation, but responded with, "Pleased to meet you, Mr Pickle."

"I'm glad you've met the Watts' boys, William. They were too young to volunteer for Gallipoli, but now they'll do their bit for England. They're ever so enthusiastic."

"Australia," Berenger corrected him curtly.

"Australia! Yes, they'll do their bit for Australia," Mr Pickle corrected himself.

"Their mother was ever so worried. It took all our convincing to get her to sign her consent. It really did."

Discerning that although Mr Pickle read Latin but probably did not read Greek, Berenger took a deep breath.

"*The etymology of the word 'enthusiasm' is religious fervour resulting from divine inspiration without the application of reason. Their mother was right to be worried,*" Berenger thought.

"Enthusiasm will get them killed," he said.

He turned abruptly and marched out through the side door to search for his company commander, hoping his contempt was not too obvious.

***

Berenger found Major Meyer in a large tent serving as one of the messes, which displayed above the entrance an official sign in black letters, the motto of 43 Battalion, '*Nil Desperandum*' (Never Despair).

Rather, it was Major Meyer who found Berenger and breaking protocol asked him if he would be permitted to eat at the senior non-commissioned officers' table as he would be able to deliver his brief during lunch. Berenger stood for the company commander and accordingly invited Major Meyer to sit with him as a *fait accompli*.

Berenger noticed a murmur amongst the many men who filed-in. The marquee was Spartan compartmentalised into separate divisions for warrant officers and senior non-commissioned officers, junior non-commissioned officers and private soldiers, who occupied the bulk of the space. The officers messed in a different smaller marquee and as such it was something of a surprise to see Major Meyer in the Other Ranks' mess.

Berenger observed ruddy-faced young braggarts grandiosely recount exploits of their conquests to their ruddier-faced even younger peers, inadvertently revealing virginity rather than virility.

Second and third sons of families, whose first sons lay anonymously as part of the glorious dead and unaccounted for at Gallipoli sat between surly men from outback Broken Hill and sickly-looking hopeful recruits, who had been turned down in New South Wales and Victoria.

Confident uniformed men, who had served in the Adelaide Rifles, sat elbows-on-tables, surveying their surroundings through furrowed eyebrows. Table-upon-table of ex-school cadets sat rigidly; many in cadet school uniforms representing their schools, eyes low, quietly and deliberately masticating their food, whilst trying to avoid eye contact with anyone older and in their minds more senior them.

Here, an eager young man trying to prove his worth to his peers or himself. There another, romantically desperate for the affections of an attractive girl; and yet another in the wake of an unhappy marriage trying to escape a fishwife.

The most dangerous, Berenger thought was the jingoist. The jingoist, who without intellectually discriminating the derring-do published in the newspapers could be manipulated into a sociopath.

Berenger felt the raw troops of the 43rd were not of the same standard as the *Fighting 10th* South Australian battalion, with whom he had departed Australia in 1915, but then he felt that those who entered the battle first would usually be the best.

This brought to mind the question why the Australian 3rd Infantry Brigade, which had had the least opportunity to train as a brigade was thrown first onto the beaches at Gallipoli. Although Berenger did not admit that New South Welshmen were better than South Australians, the famed 1st Australian Infantry Brigade had more time to train together, and therefore, in Berenger's opinion should have been accorded the honour of opening the assault.

The problem caused Berenger much mental consternation and memories of that meddling incompetent, Captain de Wet with whom Berenger had crossed paths and metaphorically crossed swords ever since they had first met in the Boer war.

Surely, that scheming vindictive de Wet could not have had any effect upon the decision-making of major-general Bridges to land the 9th Queensland battalion, the 10th South Australian battalion, the 11th Western Australian battalion, and the plucky 12th Tasmanians of the 3rd Infantry Brigade, first on the beaches of Gallipoli.

"Hmmm," Berenger muttered to himself.

"Unless," he thought, *"the mission of 3rd Infantry Brigade was to establish a foothold on the beach and the*

immediate hills, and for the 1st and 2nd infantry brigades to push through to the Dardanelles."

Berenger was still unconvinced. Why then had the heralded Lance Corporal R and Private B penetrated so deeply into the peninsula, if they had been told to establish a foothold? The answer became obvious to him: they hadn't been told to secure the beach.

Many of the men of the *Fighting 10th* South Australian battalion, like Berenger were of German descent. It was not unreasonable to suspect that some considerable effort had been made in Sydney and Melbourne into predicting that casualties from a seaborne assault would be heavy. Heavier still if they had landed in the right place. The sons of the English middle-classes in New South Wales and Victoria were more politically valuable than the sons of German South Australians (at least when state casualty lists were reported in the Sydney *Mail* and the Melbourne *Argus*).

The rear of the Division would still be the 3rd Australian Infantry Brigade in Lemnos if the 1st and 2nd Australian Infantry Brigades were to open the land battle. However, the rear would be in the West rather than in the East if the 3rd Brigade remained at Lemnos. The 3rd Brigade would not have moved and would be able to continue training until required. Training could directly ameliorate the problems experienced by the more prepared 1st and 2nd Brigades upon landing at Gallipoli and incorporated into the 3rd Brigade whilst they were held in reserve.

"At least the South Australian Advertiser had the penchant for burying the names of casualties after the advertisements in a plethora of euphemisms," Berenger thought cynically to himself.

William's father's friend, Hermann H, the Attorney General of South Australia had been forced to resign at the point of a bayonet. British Australians no longer wanted to work with German Australians and some German Australian families found voluntary internment more enticing than starving on the streets of Adelaide or becoming victims to an ever more vicious mob.

Berenger was feeling particularly resentful towards the British Empire when he happened to spy upon a 43 Battalion aboriginal recruit, head bent down, eyes low, making eye contact with no one.

The sight of an indigenous Australian soldier brought back the memory of Wiremu's sacrifice. "*As an outsider, if you want to play a part in the political future of your country, then you must fight for it,*" William thought.

"Ha, that's the spirit," he said to himself out loud.

"What's that?" exclaimed Major Meyer.

"Nothing, Sir. Just observing the general enthusiasm of the men."

Just then, Berenger's eyes caught a glimpse of Edward Watts flicking food at his younger brother. Revealing Edward's immaturity, a cruel streak and possibly a sense of inferiority for being born 12 minutes and 35 seconds after his elder brother, Albert. Berenger thought to himself, "*this one needs to be watched.*"

"Staff…" Major Meyer said gravely, "the battalion has at this stage, only enough boots, uniforms and equipment to fulfil the complete requirements of one company. That company is not our company. You will be in charge of supplying the troops with their equipment. The civilian employee, Mr Abrams will be in charge of requisitioning the supplies."

Major Meyer pointed to a thin, overly greying middle-aged man, with greasy hair, dressed in ill-fitting but tidy civilian attire, sitting at another table facing away from them, who upon hearing his name turned his head towards Berenger.

A stunned look of surprise followed by an ingratiating smile by Mr Avraham Abrams as he stood and cautiously approached Berenger, who accordingly stood up with the feeling one gets when one wants to embrace an old friend. The old friend, Mr Abrams cowering a little with his head approximately in line with the rank on Berenger's sleeve, both hands slightly trembling and eyeing a genuine smile of recognition, said in a weak voice, extending his hand, "Hello…pleased to meet you again…Sergeant Berenger", to which he received a tirade of overdue and overworked expletives in response.

4. Berenger's Escape

Once a jolly swagman camped by a billabong
Under the shade of a coolibah tree,
He sang as he watched and waited 'til his billy boiled
You'll come a-Waltzing Matilda, with me.

Andrew 'Banjo' Paterson
(1895)

A patent for the design of a new entrenching tool was registered at the Patent Office by Mr Wilhelm Berenger, who required new streams of income to support his rapidly dwindling fortunes. His usual business as a Barrister of the Supreme Court of South Australia began to diminish in present circumstances on account of his German heritage. Despite Wilhelm Berenger's long residence in Australia, past and present clients became uncertain whether his patriotic fervour was for the Motherland or the Fatherland.

Rumours abounded in the little village of Blumberg, quietly nestled in the Adelaide Hills where the Berengers had coexisted peacefully with the British for generations. The village name, reminiscent of piquant bloom-strewn rolling hills of Prussia would soon be changed to 'Birdwood' following the *zeitgeist* of patriotic Australia; (eponymous with the British Lieutenant-General commanding the Australian and New Zealand Army Corps).

It was suggested in an official letter to Mr Wilhelm Berenger from Mrs Horace A. Pickle, President of the Adelaide Town and Country Patriotic Women's Association, that as the eminently capable 'German-Jewish' commander of the Australian 4th infantry brigade, had changed his name from Monasch; with the emphasis on the '-asch' to Monash with the emphasis on the 'Mon,' Mr Wilhelm Berenger might similarly consider a more appropriate anglophone appellation such as 'Mr William Barnes'.

Mrs Horace A. Pickle suggested a name change would champion British support for poor little Belgium against German aggression by patriotic Australian's and our plucky little New Zealand cousins, who fought for the empire against the Turks and Arabs on the Gallipoli peninsula to rid Europe of German imperialism.

In an unsigned note to the Adelaide Town and Country Patriotic Women's Association, Mr Wilhelm Berenger responded in answer to Mrs Horace A. Pickle's enquiry, whether she approved of the name 'Mr William Bach' with a hard 'ch'; and would Mrs Horace A. Pickle be so kind as to present the suggested amendment and orthography to the Association at their next official 'Patriotic Women's' meeting to which the Law Practice of Mr Wilhelm Berenger, Barrister has not yet received a reply.

Mr Abrams, the civilian Procurement Officer, (whose sophisticated business dealings were previously known to William Berenger) not only procured the raw materials for the manufacture of the new entrenching tool but also 'procured' a steel forge and contracted several smiths. 'Relatives,' originally trained as goldsmiths from Melbourne; which in a round-about way is how Mr Abrams came to gain entry into Australia, in the first place.

Berenger decided to trust this untrustworthy fellow; given that he had enough information on Mr Abrams to either send him straight back to where he came from or directly to prison. However, Mr Abams could surreptitiously and spuriously suggest to influential persons that Berenger's shrapnel injuries to his back resulted from cowardice; running from the Turks, not charging into them. This would ensure the further demise of Mr Wilhelm Berenger's presently fluctuating legal career. An intention which Berenger detected in Mr Abrams' cold smile, unsmiling eyes and soft clammy handshake.

Mr Abrams was also able to detect in Berenger's aloof expression that Berenger realised the ramifications of attempting to send him to prison, whilst both parties shook hands to all outside appearances, amicably. Their relative expressions meant that the social conventions expressed with the right hand were subverted by metaphorical daggers held behind their backs with their left.

Their faces were ingratiatingly menacing to the extent that only they knew that they were capable of causing each other irreparable harm, giving them satisfaction that their commercial enterprise was more likely to be successful.

The little factory was located near the sandhills between Glenelg and Henly and embarked on producing entrenching tools to be distributed amongst 43 Battalion. The absence of the Pattern 08 entrenching tool, which had yet to be supplied by the Department of Defence was noted by the Regimental Quartermaster with concern.

Berenger whose preoccupation was to supply his company with sufficient equipment gradually issued uniforms in an unofficial *pro tempore* capacity as items arrived in his store until the company was fully supplied. He occupied the Watts' boys as suppliers to the platoon sergeants, whose stores' demands for exchanges or lost or damaged property arrived at an ever-increasing rate.

3456 Albert Watts enlisted into 43 Battalion as a regular corporal and 3465 Edward Watts as a regular lance corporal. They both beamed with pride when 3848 Lachlan Watts was finally accepted into the Battalion as a regular private soldier.

There had been a postponement in Private Watts' enlistment due to a deficiency in his administration whereby the date of birth on his birth certificate could not be correctly ascertained. A smudge over the last number of Watts' date of birth apparently caused by his mother's anguished tears when signing her consent did not with certainty verify Watts' age.

This necessitated consultation with 3848 Lachlan Watts' Latin school-master from Jesus-on-the-Torrens Charitable Public School for Boys, Mr Horace A. Pickle, who in *loco parentis* corroborated that Lachlan George Watts was born in 1897 not 1899.

This minor fact had not escaped Berenger, who intended to retain the Watts' boys as storemen to keep them away from German artillery fire for as long as possible before being better trained. Instead of confronting the boys directly, which he knew all three would lie through their teeth he quietly asked his Procurement Officer, Mr Abrams if he would investigate the *bona fides* of Jesus-on-the-Torrens Charitable Public School for Boys, Latin school-master, Mr Horace A. Pickle.

Mr Abrams without saying, 'yes' or 'no', but in reply asked whether Berenger would mind already if he would entertain advising the troops from Major Meyer's company, when they found 'abandoned' 43 Battalion military equipment. The equipment could complement their company store until its proven owner could identify and uplift the item; and of course account to their company quartermaster why they had lost it in the first place.

Both Staff Sergeant Berenger and Mr Abrams said nothing but momentarily stared blankly at each other before going about their business. In the following weeks the Watts' boys found all sorts of scarce military-issue items and secured them in the company store after which the items were distributed to C Company until each soldier had a full complement of uniform and equipment and the company store retained a modest surplus for exchanges.

Berenger generally turned a blind eye to 'abandoned' military issue stores arriving unconventionally until one day a non-issue knife engraved with its owner's regimental number appeared, whereby all three of the Watts' boys were given a cuffing and a good talking to.

They were told in no uncertain terms to find the owner of the knife by going to the battalion administration unit to compare the regimental number inscribed on the handle with regimental records. At this time, a tear welled-up in the palpebral conjunctiva (more commonly known as the lower eyelid) of 3848 Lachlan Watts' left eye.

As Berenger's piercing lecture about theft of personal property began to sink-in, the tear brimmed over and found a path down Lachlan's ruddy-red cheek. 3465 Edward Watts let out a little snigger. Both 3848 Watts and 3465 Watts received an extra cuffing from Berenger.

They were told not to rest until the item had been returned to its owner. Berenger would draft a minute to Major Meyer and Lance Corporal Watts would be invited back to the company store to uplift his new rank – Private.

***

"There have been issues arising about the *provenance* of some of the equipment in your store, Staff," Major Meyer said with concern slightly emphasising the word, 'provenance'.

Staff Sergeant Berenger stood at attention, hands firmly at his sides, feeling for the seams of his trousers and saying nothing. Major Meyer studied Berenger's minute recounting the allegations against the Watts' boys.

"They have been training well. Reports from their platoon commander are that they are all very eager," he murmured to himself.

"But this behaviour of procuring the possessions of another unlawfully is a very grave offence," he said peering over the top of the minute he had been reading, barely concealing a smile.

"I will report to the Commanding Officer, Lieutenant Colonel G. I think he will not be impressed with either you or Lance Corporal Watts," Major Meyer continued.

"Lance Corporal Watts will be demoted to the rank of private; you detach that ridiculous 10 Battalion purple-over-light-blue shoulder flash you've been sporting. Sew the correct 43 Battalion colours of brown-over-light-blue onto your tunic," he said brusquely.

A pause, whilst Berenger uncharacteristically lowered his eyes from a 45-degree angle to look at Major Meyer, whose eyes had busied themselves in the minute whilst he considered what to say next. The last physical residue of Berenger's association with the old *Fighting 10th*, his shoulder flash had to be removed forthwith.

"You and Watts can sew on your new accoutrements this evening. Now get out of my sight!"

"Sir," Berenger said in a low-pitched voice.

Rather than reveal that the slight had emotionally hurt him, Berenger saluted turned right and marched past the stone-faced platoon commanders back to the Pavilion. Less than 100 yards later, he heard hoots of laughter coming from Major Meyer's tent.

Berenger told the two younger Watts boys to retire to their cots behind a curtain made from a blanket in the company store. Berenger and 3456 Corporal Albert Watts would discuss how to deal with the younger Watts' boys.

"Lachlan is not particularly mature, Albert. He has a weak constitution for an 18-year-old," Berenger said, in a way that Albert Watts realised Berenger knew Lachlan was only 16.

"I should have a talk with him, Staff," Albert answered seriously.

Berenger did not expect Albert to concede that Lachlan was underage: a misplaced loyalty Berenger feared they would all come to regret.

Berenger then prepared them both strong mugs of steaming hot coffee to keep them awake; the blend of which was gratefully 'procured' by Mr Abrams. Before the first sip, Berenger clinked his metal cup with Albert, who beamed in response.

Both set upon a strategy of corrective training for the younger Watts' boys. Albert finished Lachlan's plan shortly thereafter and retired to bed. Berenger worked deep into the night but upon hearing the laugh of a kookaburra from a distant gumtree, he realised dawn would soon be upon him. Considering that an hour or two of sleep was better than no sleep at all, he also retired to bed.

***

After a hearty breakfast the following morning at the 43 Battalion parade consisting of a total complement of over 1000 officers and men, the battalion was called to attention by the Regimental Sergeant Major. Standing the men at-ease, the commanding officer Lieutenant Colonel G addressed his troops.

"On this day, eight months ago, one of our brave soldiers escaped from Kilitbahir prison on the Gallipoli peninsula and led his men through enemy territory safely back to the ANZAC lines. We will commemorate this achievement by conducting a 26-mile route march through undulating dunes and back to Morphettville. We will start at noon and you will march through the hottest part of the day and into the cool of the evening. Anyone, who does not complete this part of the training will at a later stage…do it again."

Staff Sergeant Berenger anonymously stood at attention, heels together, legs braced, back straight, stomach sucked-in, arms rigid, chest out, chin up.

The words, again evoked the memory of Wiremu, whom Berenger could not under any construction be said to have been led safely back to ANZAC lines...because Wiremu in No Man's Land had been killed.

Lieutenant Colonel G. paused and inspected the faces of the men in the front rank of the battalion, company-upon-company, platoon-upon-platoon. He could feel great pride in these men and great sadness too, knowing that many of these men could soon be killed. An uncharacteristic lump grew in his throat.

In the penultimate hours before this testing phase of training, Lieutenant Colonel G. believed that not every man would complete this test on the first attempt. Some of the old soldiers who'd previously served in the Adelaide Rifles thought that the battalion would suffer more than 25% casualties, (especially from the ex-cadets, whom they regarded as particularly soft).

Lieutenant Colonel G. composed himself. The battalion was somewhat bewildered as to whom this brave soldier was, who'd escaped the Turks at Gallipoli and led his men through enemy territory safely back to ANZAC lines. The two eldest Watts's boys had a fair idea although 3848 Lachlan Watts did not as yet have an inkling.

He had turned white as a ghost at the revelation that the battalion would pack-march a marathon through the sand dunes in the heat of a South Australian late summer. The scorching sun and energy sapping wind would cause the weakest soldiers to fail; and Lachlan Watts had counted himself as a weak soldier.

"The 26-mile route march shall be called..." Lieutenant Colonel G. dramatically paused, "Berenger's Escape!"

43 Battalion gasped. Lieutenant Colonel G. handed over the parade to his Regimental Sergeant Major.

"What an adventurer!" grumbled a company quartermaster from another company, who suspected some items of military equipment had been purloined by those Watts' boys.

Berenger began to feel extremely uncomfortable. In reality, he wanted to retreat into his Q Store. In present circumstances standing correctly at attention, he was not permitted to move without being dismissed by the Regimental Sergeant Major.

The Regimental Sergeant Major as if sensing Berenger's discomfort in the most stentorian voice, which could be almost be heard at Glenelg, thunderously issued the command, "Battalion...shun!"

"Battalion...Fall...out!"

In unison the battalion turned right, marched away three paces and organised themselves into companies under their company sergeants major then platoons under their sergeants returning to their company and platoon officers to be briefed on Berenger's Escape.

"A victory for battalion morale," the Regimental Sergeant Major congratulated his commanding officer.

He had observed and sensed the pride of the men with a hero of Gallipoli serving in the 43rd.

All the companies returned to their accommodations to prepare. 'A' Company, the senior company in 43 Battalion took over the battalion mess, posting guards at the entrance. All the equipment, every item must be accounted for both before and after the route march. God forbid that A Company would squirrel away extra items just in case a careless soldier may happen to lose a small piece of their rifle cleaning equipment and be deducted time points at the end.

C Company, of which Berenger who quickly wiped the saline from his face, marched directly to his quartermaster's store to compose himself, where he had previously invited the company to assemble before the day's events.

The Watts' boys, enamoured with their company quartermaster could not do enough in preparing the store and its immediate surroundings to receive the 100 or so men.

"Room!" Berenger called as Major Meyer entered the company quartermaster's store.

Crammed with nervous soldiers spilling to the outer surrounds, all stood fast for Major Meyer as he squeezed through the throng.

"Carry on, Staff," said Major Meyer as he saluted his quartermaster in reply; a wry type of smile extending to the corner of his mouth.

The C Company men went about preparing their kit for the marathon.

"3465 Edward Watts come here," ordered Berenger.

"Yes, staff," came the voice containing a tinge of 'I know I'm in trouble now'.

"Behind the curtain. Sit down," said Berenger.

Edward Watts sat down somewhat nervously. Berenger sensed that getting into trouble as a child was how Edward Watts realised his own sentience in the struggle for recognition from his parents. Although bestowed with the same genetic inheritance as his elder brother Albert, Edward always felt that he never really measured up.

His delinquent attitude and the bullying of his younger brother, Lachlan made anthropological sense to Berenger; exacerbated in a society where inheritance was conferred on the eldest son only. Edward's father's estate would pass to

Albert *in toto*, leaving Edward and Lachlan to survive on their own wits or financially at the mercy of Albert. Lachlan, situated by fate and circumstances was the unfortunate recipient of Edward's displaced frustrations.

Berenger drew his chair closer to Edward Watts. Uncharacteristically using Edward's first name he said, "Edward, if the ties between the men in the company are not as strong as the bonds between brothers, men will die and the company will fail. Lachlan, whatever his shortcomings is your brother and yet you give him less respect than any of the other men in the company."

Edward looked at the floor, grasping his knees but saying nothing. There was a moment of silence. Berenger noticed him take a deep breath an emit a kind of sigh.

"Edward, Lachlan looks up to you," Berenger said.

"If Lachlan does not finish the marathon pack march, I want you to do it again with him," Edward stared blankly at the ground.

"We have only a week before retesting. I don't know if I can recover in time. If Lachlan fails the first time, he will have little chance of passing the second time," Edward eventually answered rather plaintively.

"Edward, Albert and I will also suffer at your side," Berenger said in a quiet voice.

Gesticulating that 3465 Watts could now go, Edward Watts responded with, "Yes, staff," stood up and disappeared from behind the curtain to prepare his kit with the other men.

Berenger sat in his chair for a moment. He paused to think of himself at 18. He had disobeyed his own father, whose designs for him to enter the Boer War as an officer in the Mounted Rifles went astray when Berenger allowed his horse to die on the journey by sea from South Australia to South Africa.

In the since maligned Lieutenant Harry "Breaker" Morant, Berenger's superior officer of the Bushveldt Carbineers, he found a professional soldier, whom he wanted to emulate.

But that was all before the 'incident,' as Berenger recalled it. "Breaker" Morant was convicted and executed within 18 hours of trial of being found guilty of killing Boer prisoners. "*Very nasty business*," Berenger thought.

His mind drifting back to the veldt some 15 years ago, where often he would lie in bed at night wistfully looking at the moon and seditiously wishing he could fight for the Boer commandos himself.

Berenger respected the strength of Boer leadership. If you were not a leader, then the Boer would not follow you: very much unlike that incompetent, Captain de Wet serving as an officer in the Bushveldt Carbineers.

The words, 'No Right of Appeal' stuck in Berenger's craw. The execution of "Breaker" Morant struck him as the result of a political decision, not a judicial one. It was as if the execution of one Australian officer was meant to atone for the whole British concentration camp system, starving innocent Boer women and children to death.

It had seemed to Berenger that the South Australians were 'doing the dirty work' for the British Empire and then paying for it with their lives.

Called to the colours to fight for the Empire again at Gallipoli, this time around Berenger was adamant he was fighting for Australia.

Berenger stood up, walked purposefully around the curtain into Q Store.

"I make it, 10:45 a.m. Unless there are any questions from the platoon sergeants before I hand you back to your platoon commanders…Go!" he said.

The crescendo of rushing about was quashed by the sergeants and anxious private soldiers were calmed by their slightly older corporals as the company conducted preparations for Berenger's Escape.

At noon, the starting gun signalled the commanding officer to step off, followed by a rather over-confident A Company. A further five companies followed with the battalion colour party after the second company with colours flying. They all conducted a circuit of Morphettville race-course before embarking on their marathon 26-mile route march through the dunes at Glenelg and a final circuit of Morphettville race-course to finish.

As the battalion left the racecourse and marched down the road towards the sea, families cheered-on their sons and pretty South Australian girls coyly waved at the young men causing A company to proudly pick-up an unsustainable pace within the first mile. Berenger cynically smiled at the Watts' boys and said, "We'll all pay for that."

The temperature was over 40 degrees Celsius and rising. There was no shade for the duration but for the setting sun, which was hours away. By the time the battalion had reached the beach, the first soldiers had already dropped back to hobble along as best they could with the following company.

Being constantly encouraged by the non-commissioned officers of another company did them no end of character building as they struggled through the dunes. Instead of marching along the hard sand at the water's edge, the battalion was required to navigate through the soft sand of the undulating hills causing blisters to rise and burst only to arise again.

By 4:05 p.m. the weary men of A company began to worry that the halfway point had not yet come into sight. But the battalion flag guarded by the medics was tucked into the dunes and could only be seen by almost stepping on it.

Many of the ex-cadets were helping each other as they had been cobbers at school. Old school rivalries were soon forgotten as they knew they were all required to complete Berenger's Escape to gain any respect from the men, who had enlisted from the Adelaide Rifles.

The Adelaide Rifles had become all but silent in their suffering. Several of the older soldiers had furnished incomplete documentation to the battalion medical officers on enlistment on the promise that confirmation of their dates of birth or pre-existing medical conditions "were coming".

Men, who failed army selection in New South Wales and Victoria hung on by the skin of their teeth. There was no skin left on their feet and there were no more second chances. Boys, too young to join the *Fighting 10th* South Australian infantry battalion in 1915 assisted each other as much to prove their worth to themselves as to their mates.

As the Adelaide Rifles many of whom were in A Company rose to their weary feet, a wink from a soldier at the rear of A Company to an ex-cadet in the front rank of B Company was not missed by the Regimental Sergeant Major. He had not rested but marched up and down the files of men assessing their physical condition.

The Regimental Sergeant Major marched in "blood-soaked boots" (as was to be recorded in Battalion history) to the front rank of A Company and said to the Commanding Officer in a voice loud enough to be heard by both A and B Companies that the men were coming together nicely as a battalion.

The march back to Morphettville Racecourse was agony. For the men swept up by the hot dry wind from the Simpson Desert this was the closest experience to Hell they had yet experienced. They were yet to realise at the Western Front, they would experience far worse. Sand permeated socks to grind beneath toenails, which lifted from swollen toes. Webbing, light at the outset became an albatross around the neck rubbing off flesh at every painful step. By now, most of the men had become deathly silent as they slogged through the fine Adelaide sand.

By 5:00 p.m. the giant glowing orb of the sun still shone high in the sky and lost just a little of its scorching heat. Not a man had as yet fallen out and even the Regimental Sergeant Major and his Colour Party were struggling, but stoically marched on. Weary men trudged on to the road that would lead them back to Morphettville.

"Come on, boys!" growled a gritty captain.

"Keep going, men! Think of South Australia!" came the words of a 19-year-old second lieutenant, recently relocated to Morphettville from living with his mother.

At the junction, where the beach met the road families waving Union Jacks cheered the men-on. Young men, who had looked worse-for-wear five minutes ago inflated their chests and smiled at pretty South Australian girls as they marched past.

Not a man had dropped out but many had dropped back, now exerting themselves to reunite with their companies with less than a few miles to go. The sun was finally beginning to set and the men could anonymously reveal the agony in their faces as the darkness gradually began to enclose them.

Morphettville Racecourse was just a whisper away but still a million miles for those who thought they had nothing left. Somewhere in the middle of the battalion the strains of a familiar song wafted through the air.

Edward saw his younger brother struggling. Lachlan had stopped perspiring. His eyes were glazed. Edward sensed Lachlan would fall at any moment.

"Once a jolly swagman camped by a billabong," the breathless Private Edward Watts sang. Lachlan, looking at Edward grimaced and resolutely joined in, "Under the shade of a coolibah tree."

With the strides of bleeding feet stepping out and a wink from Edward at Lachlan, almost the whole of C Company joined in with, "He sang as he watched and waited 'til his billy boiled." Giving inspiration to the whole battalion when the words were heard by the commanding officer leading the 43rd and the last men at the rear of the battalion, all joined in, "You'll come a-Walzing Matilda with me."

By the time they approached the gates of Morphettville Racecourse near the 8:30 p.m. cut-off time the crowds had grown larger and larger. Children, waving Union Jacks skipped along singing next to the soldiers. Handkerchiefs belonging to pretty South Australian girls, (with perhaps a message of support) surreptitiously disappeared into the pockets of soldiers not having come to the attention of their ever-vigilant sergeants; or so they thought.

Through the gates 43 Battalion proudly marched their final circuit of Morphettville Racecourse to the crescendo of:

"Waltzing Matilda, Waltzing Matilda
You'll come a-Waltzing Matilda, with me
He sang as he watched and waited 'til his billy boiled,
you'll come a-Waltzing Matilda, with me!"

The following morning the battalion medical facility was inundated with aches, strains and general injuries suffered from Berenger's Escape.

"How many men are here, who served with the Adelaide Rifles?" enquired the Regimental Sergeant Major.

The short answer, given tersely but respectfully by the battalion senior medical officer before he rushed off the treat yet another twisted knee was, "Almost all of 'em."

5. Going to the Chapel

"Dearly beloved, we are gathered here today in the sight of God to join this man and this woman in holy matrimony. Not to be entered into lightly, holy matrimony should be entered into solemnly and with reverence and honour."

...and if Staff Sergeant Berenger wasn't busy enough, Juliana had been behaving surprisingly strange of late. Her usual fortitude interspersed with unforgettable little moments of humour, which courting couples often experience at the outset of their relationship was substituted with moodiness and tearful outbursts. Conduct, which William could not for the life of him understand.

Juliana had spurned William's attempts to show affection by sometimes holding both her hands and looking at her when he was talking. But Juliana appeared to be in no mood for eye contact and often turned her back or busied herself with some domestic duty when William attempted to communicate.

William was allowed leave from Morphettville on some weekends and they often spent time alone together walking along the beach. The walks became more and more silent and both William and Juliana buried in their thoughts began to drift ever so slightly apart.

Miss Fischer, born and bred in Adelaide had surrendered herself into an internment camp on Torrens Island on account of Mr Wilhelm Berenger having neither clients nor money to pay for her services. Mr Wilhelm Berenger had decided to take up with Mr Avraham Abrams in the production of entrenching tools in anticipation of a contract with the Australian Department of Defence.

Despite the long hot summer nights in Adelaide the atmosphere at William's cottage had become decidedly frosty. Juliana had taken up duties as a housekeeper for a modest stipend from Wilhelm Berenger and she handled William's frugal finances.

To save money Juliana had left lodgings in Adelaide and occupied the room vacated by Miss Fischer and on occasion occupied another room: the one in which, William slept.

One evening, whilst Juliana was cooking dinner and William was at the kitchen table she said exasperatedly, "William, I am with child."

William froze. A bewildered expression came over his face. Regarding Juliana's desperate outburst, he awkwardly exclaimed, "How?"

For the first time in their courtship, Juliana's face screwed up and she started crying. She ran out of the kitchen, slamming the door behind her. An immediate ejaculation for lack of circumspect William was already beginning to rue. He followed her outside and caught up with her. Juliana stood sullenly, weeping on the veranda.

He took a large gulp of air, embraced Juliana and said, "I am sorry I said that. I love you, honey."

Juliana's weeping reduced to sobs as the large kangaroo on the hill with family in tow, silhouetted by the setting sun hopped closer. Juliana rested her head on William's shoulder watching these strange marsupials intently. When a little joey popped her head out of her mother's pouch to investigate, Juliana simultaneously let out a little laugh and a little cry and William led her back into the house to turn off the lights.

The following weekend, the Watts' boys spent Saturday tidying up the gardens of Berenger's cottage. William busied himself inside making sure everything was clean and tidy. He paid special attention to a bouquet that was placed on the kitchen table as a centrepiece for a formal dinner.

Juliana was away in town on some domestic errands and William would surprise her with a lovely dinner. He had studied the correct way to set the table and unconventionally set the salt-cellar at Juliana's end of the table. It signified that whilst they were at home Juliana would be head of the household.

He had taught Lachlan Watts how to correctly fold a napkin. William decided on service à la russe where all dishes would be laid out simultaneously on a second-hand dumb waiter. He selected five plates that looked approximately the same and placed them around the dinner table.

To differentiate the entrée fork from the fish fork and mains fork – all the same-sized forks – William placed three forks beside each other for dramatic effect and set about arranging knives and spoons on the other side of the plate.

A candelabra was offset from a more important and intentionally empty space. That would symbolise where the beautiful Delft pitcher Juliana's mother, Cornelia would have displayed it had it not been broken by the vindictive de Wet in K-concentration camp in the Boer war.

When Juliana arrived home at about 4:00 p.m. she was greeted sheepishly by William. She gasped when she discerned the meaning of the space on the table in remembrance of her mother Cornelia.

William led Juliana to her seat and the Watts boys joined them. After a few brief speeches from William and Albert Watts, Juliana offered an extemporary reply and a prayer. The food all tasted delicious even in the manner that the Watts boys consumed it with dessert and main all going on the same plate. Juliana did not mind, and William was more amused than bemused when Lachlan Watts started to dip portions of meat into his soup with his fingers.

The conversation was convivial until sunset when the candelabra was lit. The light flickered upon the faces of Juliana and the boys in the same way that the light flickered upon the Delft pitcher in Cornelia's little tent in camp K. William's eyes welled up with the memory and Juliana coyly inclined her head down, but their eyes remained locked.

"Gentlemen, would you be so kind as to excuse us for a moment," William asked the Watts' boys, who rose and tucking in their chairs retired outside to the veranda. William stood up, approached Cornelia and went down on one knee.

Ultimately, a victory for Juliana's dead mother. Cornelia had sacrificed herself and all her children to save her eldest daughter. Unbeknownst to Juliana, Cornelia had subdivided their meagre rations in camp K; and so that Juliana could survive. Juliana's younger brothers Johannes, Peter Lambertus, and younger sisters Geertje and Magdalena had all starved to death.

Juliana pressed both hands to her heart in expectation. Tears streamed down William's face. The Watts' boys had left the veranda and gone around the side of the house to peer through the kitchen window behind William. As the window was too high for any of the boys to peer through, Juliana caught a whisper from Lachlan to his brothers, "You'll just have to carry me."

William noticed that Juliana's eyes had ever so briefly drawn their attention to the window and back to him.

"Juliana. Will you…" William looked into Juliana's eyes.

Concurrently, some discernible grunts of exertion emanated from beneath the kitchen window as 3456 and 3465 Watts lifted their brother onto their shoulders. As Lachlan exclaimed, "Carry me!" simultaneously William asked Juliana, "Marry me?"

To a vision of Lachlan Watts pressing his gormless face against the kitchen window, which again momentarily distracted Juliana she gave an unreserved, "Yes."

Instead of embracing his fiancée, William shot a filthy look over his shoulder, stood up and ran to the kitchen window. This caused Lachlan to fall back and topple on top of his brothers on the ground outside. The boys scurried away into the dark, which was followed by a tirade of expletives from the kitchen window.

On the evening that William and Juliana had expressed their commitment to each other, William's anger at the Watts boys did not last long. They were soon invited back into the house to celebrate the pending nuptials. They all toasted with a small glass of sherry except Juliana, who toasted with water not alcohol. The Watts boys felt grown-up toasting the couple with sherry, considering their previous antics.

When it was time to retire, William asked the Watts' boys to help him tidy up and respectfully asked Juliana, "Would you like to retire to *your* room, whilst we tidy up?"

A snigger from 3465 Edward Watts was quickly quashed by a stern glance by William.

On Monday, Berenger wrote a letter to his company sergeant major:

"To WO2 Becker
CSM
C Company
43 Battalion

I have a matter of extreme delicacy that I would like to bring to the attention of Major Meyer. I would like to marry my fiancée, Miss Juliana Kruger before the 43rd Battalion departs for England.

For your consideration at the soonest opportunity,

Ssgt William Berenger
Quartermaster
C Company
43 Battalion"

Sergeant Major Becker opening and reading the letter was taken aback.

"You know the rules, William," he said using William's first name in such a way that Berenger knew his response was likely to be, "No."

"However, the decision is not mine, and I will forward it to Major Meyer."

"Thank you, sir," Berenger said.

Major Meyer realised the import of the words, 'extreme delicacy,' where Company Sergeant Major Becker, who considered company discipline to be paramount did not. The letter found its way to the commanding officer, who discussed it with his Regimental Sergeant Major.

"Sir, battalion discipline is paramount. As you may be aware Berenger is not the only soldier, who has a fiancée. This will start an unpleasant precedent. If one soldier is granted permission to marry in contravention of policy it would not be unreasonable for the men to hold grievances against Berenger and disrupt battalion morale," the Regimental Sergeant Major suggested.

"Hmmm…" Lieutenant Colonel G said pensively.

"You are right. I must weigh up the benefits to the battalion and balance them with the detriments. I give weight to Berenger's present contribution to the battalion. He has designed and began to make entrenching tools. These matters are over and above his soldierly qualities, notwithstanding the questionable manner, in which he supplied his company with uniforms and equipment," he smiled to himself.

Lieutenant Colonel G nodded to his RSM, "Yes, again you are right unless there are very serious mitigating factors, it would set an unfortunate precedent. But to my mind, an unmarried mother would have less entitlement to Berenger's estate if he were killed, than if she was his widow. The fate of an unmarried fiancée with a child would be severe on both the young woman and the child." ˙

Lieutenant Colonel G continued, "There have been no other applications to date of this nature and we deploy to the Western Front very shortly. Out of loyalty to Staff Sergeant Berenger, I wish to keep the reasons for his application discrete. I allow it on grounds of meritocracy over and above duty and to encourage a spirit of meritocracy in the battalion."

"As you please, sir," said the Regimental Sergeant Major perfunctorily.

"You know…" Lieutenant Colonel G sighed, "this decision may not bode well at brigade not to mention what they will make of it at division."

The Regimental Sergeant Major responded with a few characteristic words of support.

"Thank you, RSM."

Lieutenant Colonel G was never quite sure whether this life-long soldier was making light of him but he was sure that his RSM would support his decision whether it turned out to be right or wrong.

The wedding was scheduled to be held at Morphettville. Only C Company men were invited to the ceremony. Other than the Commanding Officer and the Regimental Sergeant Major, Lieutenant Colonel G felt that although it was well known in the battalion that Berenger would marry before deploying to the Western Front. The gossip which abounded as to the identity and provenance of the young lady to whom he would be wed soon abated when a short period of battalion leave approached.

One hundred and two invitations were duly typed by 3456 Edward Watts, beginning with, "We cordially request the pleasure of your company…" Berenger, found his name misspelt as 'Berengar' on the little card, and instructed 3456 Edward Watts with one word: "Again."

Edward Watts returned to the company *Mitterhofer* typewriter with a down-turned face and a grumble. He was learning the value of getting it right.

The battalion pavilion was out-of-bounds to all but invitees on the auspicious day. However, since leave had been previously granted to the remainder of the battalion from 8:00 a.m. Morphettville was all but deserted.

'A' company had interpreted the instruction as they could take leave from 5:00 p.m. the previous evening and were all well gone. All their equipment was left in inspection order. Lieutenant Colonel G could not fault them for this creative interpretation of his order as they remained the finest performing company in the battalion.

The *trauzeuge* (witness to the marriage) was William's father. Wilhelm Berenger went to an extraordinary effort to comfort Juliana on this propitious day and as she had no living relations, he would also walk the bride down the aisle.

3456 Albert Watts and 3465 Edward Watts stood next to the groom, Mr William Berenger at the altar. Miss Fischer, stood in as bridesmaid for Juliana. She looked remarkably dignified and correctly attired considering Mr Abrams had only recently secured her release from internment on Torrens Island.

The aisle was composed of row-upon-row of benches upon which the men of C Company occupied on both sides. At the front sat the Commanding Officer, the Regimental Sergeant Major, Major Meyer, Company Sergeant Major Becker and Mr Abrams.

As Juliana and Mr Wilhelm Berenger entered the pavilion, the *hochzeitsmarsch* began to play. Mr Abrams tapped his foot in time to the music.

Juliana wore a simple wedding dress, saved and taken in by Miss Fischer, who no longer dreamed of such lofty ambitions as marriage. Miss Fischer had also helped Juliana with her long blonde hair, styling those intricate curls that she knew William liked.

"Please be seated," said the Lutheran minister.

Enigmatically, to all but William, Juliana, and Miss Fischer, he addressed the congregation.

"The wisdom of the galah," he began.

"Dearly beloved, we are gathered here today…"

6. The Regimental Dispatch Messenger

Deutschland, Deutschland über alles,
Über alles in der Welt,
Wenn es stets zu Schutz und Trutze
Brüderlich zusammenhält.
Von der Maas bis an die Memel,
Von der Etsch bis an den Belt,
Deutschland, Deutschland über alles,
Über alles in der Welt!

August Heinrich Hoffmann von Fallersleben, 1841

The *Fighting 10th* had posted spotters in the belfry of Our Lady as had their British predecessors. Given Berenger's head-wound, he decided he would no longer require his *Zeiss* binoculars whilst he convalesced. Berenger lent the binoculars to the spotters, requiring their signatures in his quartermaster's log, in expectation of their return.

Berenger refused to convalesce anywhere else but 10 Battalion HQ, which had been relocated underground in the crypt of Our Lady after a round from a German 'five-nine' caused the ceiling above the transept to come crashing down upon the nave.

He kept his kit and rifle near his cot in a dark niche concealed by an army blanket strung across his entombed space. The blanket hung in such a way as to allow both a modicum of privacy whilst admitting a sliver of lamp-light to pierce between the blanket and cold damp stone wall against which, Berenger's cot lay.

The cot consisted of two pews pushed together; one with its back against the stone wall and the other with its back removed at the bench so that Berenger could enter what could otherwise be described as a lid-less coffin.

The spotters noted the devastating accuracy of German artillery upon the 10th Battalion positions had increased daily. As the sun dipped beneath the horizon at the predicted time, intermittent enemy flares and searchlights lit up No Man's Land, again at the predicted time. When there was no artificial light any relative ambience would often be reduced to an inky opaque.

One of the spotters had visited Berenger, who was supine on his make-shift sick-bed, head towards the sliver of light so he could study a fragment of a map of Poziéres. It was hand-drawn by a previous British occupant of Our Lady marked with suspected dispositions of German trenches and machine guns.

The spotter explained the problem caused by the intermittent flashes of artificial light whilst observing No Man's Land through binoculars from the belfry. He waited patiently, standing outside Berenger's dark niche. Unconsciously wringing his hands, the spotter listened to Berenger's pained breathing and passed between the blanket and the cold stone wall as a courtesy so Berenger could better observe him.

Berenger placed the map, face down on his chest, upon which he rested his hands. He lay with his head supported by his webbing. Despite his ailing physical condition, Berenger's intellectual acuity remained intact.

Another shallow breath. Berenger's eyes, already adjusted to the relative darkness of his tomb observed a concerned corporal peering down upon him.

"Henry," Berenger began.

"Are you right-handed or left-handed?"

"Right-handed, sir."

"Close your right eye before the time you predict a flare or a search-light and the pupil will remain dilated during the evening. You may not achieve this every time but with discipline you will achieve it more than the enemy and your vision will be less impaired."

Berenger paused.

"Remember to scan the ground right to left, bottom to top for movement first, not colour. Ensure you draw the most detailed picture during the day of the ground you intend to observe during the night. Judge your distances accurately, noting any salient features. Instead of using one page from your field notebook, tape four pages together with this tape."

Berenger handed the corporal some tape he had invented. Upon the corporal's quizzical expression, Berenger showed him how to apply it.

"Your pencil illustration should be four times as detailed. Use shading appropriately. You should be able to discern at least five shades of grey from your pencil. Note the time and direction of movements and flares on a separate page with as much detail as you can. Ensure every sentry is briefed on the latest version of your ground before dusk every day; and that every sentry is briefed again by the previous sentry, whom they are to relieve. Any differences in that picture may be enemy or evidence of enemy activity."

He paused again, to consider.

"Differentiate between friend and foe by the silhouette of his *pickelhaube* or *stahlhelm*. Take an example of each of these helmets into the belfry with you and study the difference in shadow on the face between them and your Brodie Mark I using the sun in the same position during the day you observed a flare the previous evening.

I wish to collate every evening's observations. No enemy wiring parties fixing enemy obstacles suggests that there may be no obstacles. This suggests a field of fire for a machine-gun from which, I can confirm by extrapolation on my map."

Berenger held up the document to show the spotter.

The spotter's expression revealed the light of realisation. A combined sense of vigour, gravity and gratitude came over his hitherto exhausted face. With sage advice, Berenger had conferred an implied battalion objective, which was inferred with a deep gravitas. Further bolstered by recognition of his first name by his sergeant major, Henry said, "Sir," and certainly he could achieve this task, slipped back into the flickering lamp-light.

Berenger listened to the explanation of the spotter to a battalion staff officer as to what he was doing in Battalion HQ. The spotters had previously observed a German dispatch messenger momentarily appear between Australian and German trenches. To date, too quick for the battalion marksmen the messenger would sprint in short bursts, zigzagging across No Man's Land to drop into an enemy forward sap, concealed position or listening post. Liaising with the Forward Observers he relayed his messages in the absence of effective field telephone lines, which were as often blown up by their artillery as by the Australians.

Berenger, head wrapped in bandages secured by tape, (now intentionally camouflaged with mud and soot) spoke to the new acting company quartermaster 3456 Corporal Albert Watts. Albert positioned a small makeshift requisitions counter (namely, the back of one of Berenger's pews balanced upon two boxes) next to Berenger's convalescent residence.

"Find 3465 Watts, would you? I will forward a request to the Regimental Sergeant Major to speak to Lieutenant Colonel P-W that Edward and I conduct a reconnaissance mission into No Man's Land this evening."

"Sir," Corporal Watts replied as he dashed up the lamp-lit stone stairs in search of 3465 Watts.

Possession of No Man's Land depended more upon the will and ingenuity of the possessor not to relinquish it. The wounded and dying between the trenches called piteously for help. The stretcher-bearers, who slithered out of their trenches to collect the wounded men would often become casualties themselves; killed or wounded by an enemy sniper.

In the evenings wiring parties would slither out to repair wire and obstacles destroyed during the day's bombardments: an excruciatingly stressful task as the men would often have to remain completely still, (even if standing-up) during the many flares and search-lights set upon discovering them as movement would have drawn fire from the enemy trenches.

Often the wiring parties would use the protection of the sap dug by the men in the listening posts, which ran perpendicular to the front-line trench to beyond the wire entanglements.

During the night, reconnaissance parties probed the enemy for weak spots to mount an attack or enemy machine-guns posts to avoid. Berenger advised the reconnaissance parties to fire a rifle to encourage a German machine-gun to respond; thereby discovering both its position and the likely positions of flanking machine-guns given the German proclivity for mathematical accuracy in structuring their defences.

Amongst the constant nightly activity battalion runners both Australian and German bravely traversed the battlefield conveying messages often becoming the men wounded and dying, calling piteously for help.

At dusk Berenger and 3465 Edward Watts slithered over the parapet. Berenger had conducted a map reconnaissance with the spotters and the commanding officer earlier in the day. If Berenger was killed, seniority and precedence to take his place would be the platoon sergeant from 1 platoon as acting company quartermaster. 3456 Corporal Albert Watts was as yet too inexperienced. 3848 Private Lachlan Watts would replace 3465 Private Edward Watts if they both were killed.

Berenger, head throbbing would crawl from shell-hole to shell-hole. Both he and 3465 Edward Watts had firmly strapped 'Berenger's entrenching tool' to their backs and held their rifles in their arms to crawl on their elbows.

"Just in case we have to dig our way back," Berenger winked at 3465 Watts before they left their trenches.

Terrified of what he would find in No Man's Land, Edward Watts merely croaked in reply. The feeling of letting down Berenger, his brothers or his new battalion was greater than his fear of 'going over the top'.

"Good luck boy," the machine-gun corporal gruffly grunted and patted him on the back as he went over. A grateful croak and Edward Watts disappeared through a gap in the barbed wire.

Berenger viewed this task as an unavoidable duty. To Edward Watts the task was both terrifying and exhilarating. The exhilaration abated when he slithered over an eviscerated German corpse. Berenger crawled slowly and deliberately on his elbows, rifle in his hands, entrenching tool slung on his back.

Realising the merest shadow in the undulating ground would offer concealment from prying eyes under a flare, Berenger and Edward Watts slithered into a crater near enough to the German trench to form a wide field of observation, from which it was expected that the German runner would soon emerge.

Presently, two handles of a German stretcher carelessly protruded from the German trench.

"Watts, shhh," growled Berenger as he observed two German stretcher-bearers creep over the parapet. Co-ordinating his breathing with his aim both soldiers scurried in and out of Berenger's rifle sights.

"Why didn't you shoot 'em, sir?"

"Shhh, Watts," Berenger gruffly whispered.

Watts was learning the rules of war in the pragmatic but esoteric manner that non-commissioned officers often conduct instruction.

The sun had set and Berenger sensed movement in the trench to his front. Although there was scarcely any ambient light left. Sound travelled more acutely through the chill evening air. Berenger opened his mouth slightly, cocked his head, and listened to the sound of footsteps padding along creaking duck-boards in the trench opposite. He closed his mouth when the sound of footsteps stopped. More firmly resting the butt of his rifle into the flesh of his jaw, Berenger slowed his breathing.

At the briefing before his patrol, Berenger was advised by the spotters that German dispatch messengers tend not to crawl to their destinations. It is too slow. A message delivered late is of no use at all. They tended to sprint in short bounds when exposed and dive into cover between trenches. They do not read the messages they convey, so every message means life or death to a *kamerad* if it is not delivered in that urgent way that the Germans covet timeliness.

"German dispatch messengers are selected for their determination, their independence and their cunning," expostulated the 10-battalion intelligence officer as if reading from a book; unaware of Lieutenant Colonel P-W's furrowed expression.

"While they are alive, German dispatch messengers pose a high priority threat to us. If we interrupt enemy communications between their artillery and their Forward Observers, they will have less access to report our movements," the intelligence officer said, stating the obvious.

***

In a flash, a head appeared in Berenger's sights and quickly disappeared, only to appear somewhere else along the trench line. Presciently, the German dispatch messenger had replaced his *pickelhaube* with a *stahlhelm*. Otherwise, Berenger's vertical foresight would have rested silently upon the anachronistic protuberance from the German's helmet, patiently awaiting the silhouette of an anxious face to appear.

The trigger of Berenger's rifle gently squeezed would ultimately cause the hammer to strike the percussion cap of the bullet. Berenger's control over the bullet ostensibly extended, although ever so slightly to the moment between the explosion in the breech and the round leaving the muzzle. A moment so fleeting and yet so significant as to ostensibly be capable of extinguishing life, affecting the fate of armies or precipitating the rise and fall of civilisations: a moment clumsily achieved in Sarajevo by Gavrilo Princep two years and a civilisation ago.

In this instant, it was not impossible that Berenger could have acted upon latent second thoughts. An inadvertent jerk on the trigger may have sent the bullet in a slightly different direction. A mere moment's lapse in concentration may have meant a target missed. A new intervening act may have deflected the round in a different direction.

Rising ever so slightly upon its trajectory, the round no longer controlled by Berenger, once left the muzzle would strike the German dispatch messenger in his anxious face as his head rose to meet it. In this instance, this was not the case.

The dispatch messenger tentatively arose from his trench, sprinted several yards and disappeared into a shell-hole. Berenger adjusted his alignment so that now his body was parallel with the German trench from whence the dispatch messenger had first appeared. The German cautiously appeared again; and again the dispatch messenger leapt out of the shell-hole, sprinted a few yards and went to ground only a few yards from where Berenger was laying.

Edward Watts immediately devised a cunning plan, "Call him in sir," he whispered.

In the dim ambient light, Edward Watts saw a crooked smile extend along the left-hand side of Berenger's face. Watts, no longer felt terrified.

"*Sie!*" Berenger whispered in a growl. *"Kommen, sie!"*

The dispatch messenger sensing the sanctuary of a shell-hole sprinted towards Berenger and dived-in head-first, legs splayed apart. Edward Watts grabbed the sharpened steel entrenching tool like an axe and struck the flailing German in a down-ward motion between his legs with such a force that this man's scrotum tore. The spermatic cord was severed and a crushed testicle slipped out, permanently depriving this man's ability to produce children.

The German in agony sprung into Edward Watts, fingers grasping at Watt's throat and thumbs pressing into his carotid. Smelling of garlic and onions, fiery eyes piercing the German spat guttural curses into Watts' terrified face. Watts felt himself losing consciousness until Berenger tore off this man's helmet and beat him unconscious with it.

Berenger panted as he searched the unconscious messenger for documents. Leaving his Iron Cross, he snapped the identity disk retaining one half in his pocket and leaving the remaining half with the prisoner, lest he was killed before Berenger could get him to Australian-occupied lines.

When this man regained consciousness, Berenger could sense the injury to this soldier's groin was dire and he would be unable to walk. Shivering and in agony, the German and Edward Watts sat glaring at each other throughout the night.

Watts remained stock-still, weapon trained upon his foe; muzzle just out of the German's immediate reach. The German suffered in silence, right hand tightly grasping his injured groin, lifeblood and urine seeping between his fingers from his saturated uniform.

"Well done, Edward," Berenger whispered.

3465 Edward Watts felt to be called Edward was an honour indeed. To him it represented acceptance and was complemented by a nod of approval, whilst Berenger forcibly removed the German's hand and attempted to inspect his gaping wound.

Berenger noted that the muzzle of the German's Mauser had become filled with dirt as he dived into the shell hole. An egregious offence from which Berenger determined that this was not a truly vaunted battalion message dispatcher, (who carried a pistol) but a lesser regimental one. Therefore, Berenger had indeed intercepted the message dispatcher intended to convey messages to and from the Forward Artillery Observers.

Berenger removed some tape from his head; being careful not to allow the adhesive side to touch upon itself. Edward moved his position so that his rifle was trained upon the prisoner, whilst Berenger cleaned his wound. In the dark, the missing testicle could not be found.

"Probably still in his trousers," Edward whispered unhelpfully.

Berenger was impressed with this man's stoic ability to withstand pain. He carefully sealed the scrotum of his prisoner by applying the tape to secure the dressing in place. During the procedure, the prisoner arched his back in agony and slumped unconscious.

Shortly, before the sun rose on the longest night of Edward Watts' life, Berenger and Watts left this gravely wounded German to be rescued by his stretcher-bearers. Unloading his Mauser, they dug it into the ground, muzzle first at the German side of the shell hole as a daytime marker for both the spotters in the belfry and the German stretcher bearers, who would try to rescue him.

Leaving him a water canteen, they slithered out of the shell hole, but not before Berenger patted the little *gefreiter* on the shoulder and said in German rather enigmatically, "This too shall pass."

The fire of hatred and agony burning in the *gefreiter's* eyes momentarily abated. By the time Berenger and Watts had negotiated their way back to Australian lines, it was already almost dawn. The German sat sullenly, sometimes conscious, sometimes unconscious stoically awaiting his fate: water bottle untouched.

Berenger whispered the password to the Australian machine-gunner, who beckoned them through. Marching directly back to the crypt of Our Lady. In anticipation of the debrief, he assembled the notes and the property he had taken on his makeshift cot by the sliver of light piercing between the cold stone wall and the blanket.

The message appeared to indicate that there was a tunnel beneath No Man's Land leading from Our Lady but that the Germans had not yet located it. Due to the tunnel's significance to the Germans, the message indicated, "be vigilant for the tunnel when they moved positions." Berenger translated the short-hand on his half of the identity disk as, 'Bavarian Reserve Infantry Regiment 16', obliquely noted the name as, 'Adolf Hitler' and returned the disk to his tunic pocket.

***

C Company, 43 Battalion were shipped out of Adelaide as reserves for the *Fighting 10th*, who were soon to be situated approximately south-west of Pozières either side of the Baupame Road around the village of Albert.

Lieutenant Colonel G believed they were the best-trained company that he could afford to send directly to the Western Front; to the consternation of the A company men, who returned to Morphettville after Christmas leave. To a man, A company believed they were the best company in the battalion and that they should have had the honour of deploying as the first reserves to the 10th South Australian Battalion.

They had all looked very glum when they heard the news at the first-morning battalion parade of 1916 until their company sergeant major permitted to them run circuits around Morphettville Racecourse so they could all cheer-up again, which wasn't until about midday when they were all too exhausted to be glum.

Staff Sergeant Berenger received two letters after he delivered his brief at 10 Battalion HQ: one from Mr Abrams and one from Juliana. Wanting to keep Juliana's letter for the evening, he opened Mr Abrams' letter first:

"To Ssgt William Berenger
A/CSM
C Company
10 South Australian Battalion
Dear Staff Sergeant Berenger,

I have some news from the Patent Office. The design and contract for our new entrenching tool has been accepted by the Australian Department of Defence.

There was another design, with which I was impressed. The entrenching tool was made of similar steel to ours but the head folded in. Adjacent to the head was a pick, which also folded in. I think we were fortuitous, that our design was accepted.

I discovered that the inventor was a woman. When the Adelaide Town and Country Patriotic Women's Association discovered the gender of the inventor, they petitioned the Patent Office against it.

I also discovered that the 9th Queensland Battalion has been credited with being the first ashore at the Gallipoli landings. They have not decided whether it was either Major R, Lieutenant C, or Lance Sergeant S but the Queenslanders are adamant that it was at 4:28 a.m.

Juliana is doing well.
Warm Regards,
Avraham Abrams
43 Battalion
Procurement Officer"

The news regarding the *Fighting 9th* Queensland infantry battalion claim brought back a fond memory of big Tom, the feisty Queenslander. Always up for a fight Tom, who along with Berenger and six others escaped from the Turks at Gallipoli.

Boldly breaking free from Fort Kilitbahir, Berenger decided that two parties of four would have a greater chance of slipping through the Turkish lines back to the New Zealand trenches than one party of eight. He selected Tom to lead the three Queenslanders and they parted their ways on the eastern side of the Gallipoli peninsula. Berenger was unaware of how Tom and his men managed to make it back alive.

Berenger, Ali, Kuehn and Wiremu travelled at night, made several unsuccessful attempts at slipping through the Turkish lines before finally finding themselves slithering through No Man's Land after an act of sophisticated subterfuge. With only yards left to crawl to the New Zealand trenches, the four men, who had further divided into two pairs were spotted by the Turks.

Wiremu sacrificed himself by standing up, drawing enemy fire originally intended for all of them. Wiremu was killed in No Man's Land. The constant burden of self-blame has plagued Berenger ever since.

In any event, Berenger was glad for big Tom for the honour bestowed upon the Queensland battalion. If Berenger only knew that Private Thomas Balfour was at present still fighting for his life in a military hospital in England, he would have at least arranged to send him a telegram.

Berenger was unaware that on the 19th of May 1915, big Tom was shot by the Turks, eventually losing almost half his face. This recklessly brave young man had clambered up onto the parapet firing his last round into the enemy and charged headfirst, bayonet at the ready into an oncoming swarm of Turkish soldiers. So much blood spewed forth from the blast to his face that the Turks thought they had killed him where he fell.

Tom's mates, seeing their fallen comrade also rose upon the parapet to repel an attack of such violence that when the last Turks had turned and fled, Tom was buried three deep in Turkish bodies, with many of his brave comrades loyal to the bitter end, dead around him.

But the Queensland battalion held.

***

Berenger passed between the blanket dividing his nook in the crypt where he slept. He lay on two pews pushed together to form an uncomfortable cot and began to read Juliana's letter.

"To my darling husband,

I am not well. The doctor says there will be some difficulties with my present condition. But I am safe in Adelaide and Miss Fischer has been such wonderful help.

The plumbing under the sink is leaking…"

Head throbbing, Berenger momentarily closed his eyes. He awoke with a start to see Edith bending over him, as ethereal as ever.

"I'm sorry, I woke you up, sir. I am just here to check your dressing."

Edith moved her lamp closer to William's head. William could see her naked breasts pressing against her habit. Deciding not to give in to inappropriate thoughts, he turned his head and eyes away. But the thoughts had already implanted themselves in his mind.

"I did not hear you enter, Edith," William said talking to the cold stone wall.

"I did not want to wake you, William," was her gentle reply.

"William, your dressing is difficult to change. It appears to have adhered to your head." Edith touched William's wound.

"Excuse me, William, while I get some solvent to remove your dressing," Edith apologised.

A brief "Argh" came from Berenger's mouth. He turned his head but both the lamp and Edith had disappeared. Berenger overheard a muffled conversation where the 3rd Brigade would again be thrown into battle to break through the German lines at Pozières.

"3 Brigade again. Typical," Berenger thought.

"We have not trained properly for this type of activity," he thought but did not dare to say aloud.

Berenger did not realise then that four battalions of New South Welshmen from the highly favoured 1st Australian Brigade would be sent into the cauldron with them. Nor was he apprised of the more than 5000 casualties incurred by the Australian 5th Division recently at Fromelles. He would have been cynically unsurprised that the Germans had learnt of the attack at La Boiselle on 1 July 1916 from an intercepted British message, "Good luck for tomorrow."

He settled down to continue Juliana's letter.

"...and dripping onto the kitchen floor.

Leaves from the trees outside blow into the house through open doors and windows and cause Miss Fischer all sorts of strife sweeping them up. Miss Fischer is in such a conundrum..."

Berenger smiled at such domestic dilemmas and drifted off into a fitful sleep, wherein a fugue he noted Edith coming in from time to time to check his condition. In his sleep, a humorous notion manifested itself into Berenger's mind, which caused a guffaw. He did not dispute the Queenslanders' claim that they were first ashore at Gallipoli at 4:28 a.m. However, he did have certain reservations over whether anyone in the *Fighting 9th* Queensland infantry battalion could tell the time.

7. "Every Man Is Born As Many Men and Dies As A Single One"

I often go on bitter nights
To Wotan's oak in the quiet glade
With dark powers to weave a union —
The runic letters the moon makes with its magic spell
And all who are full of impudence during the day
Are made small by the magic formula!

German poem

Regimental Dispatch Messengers were regarded by Battalion Dispatch Messengers as less brave. The battalion dispatch messengers' short life expectancy belied their cynical perspective. When the *gefreiter* and his subordinate approached from Regimental HQ to ask for directions, observing RIR 16, (Reserve Infantry Regiment 16) on their epaulettes they were sarcastically told to go to Hell.

Often sent by their not as yet mentally unstable adjutant, *Kapitän* H, the *gefreiter* was regarded as dutiful and reliable in his work. Swallowing the battalion dispatch messengers' unhelpful advice, the two traversed further along the trench, tripping over and stumbling into soldiers from the front-line battalion presently standing-to.

They stopped approximately in line with the silhouette of the belfry of Our Lady. The Forward Observers would be located precisely 50 metres at right-angles to the trench. (The Germans had been using the metric system since the 1870s.) However, part of the trench had been recently decimated by an Australian bombardment and excavations had relocated it with a 'U' bend further back.

"Ernst," the *gefreiter* whispered in a Bavarian accent, closeting his Austrian heritage.

"I need a rifle. Distract that man." He gestured towards a soldier leaning against the parapet.

Kapitän H had admired the *gefreiter's* ability to accurately reproduce by memory, images of enemy defences around Pozières in the preceding weeks. German tunnellers and geologists by observing the *gefreiter's* sketches correctly calculated there was a water table between them and their objective. The tunnellers, freshly apprised of this information abandoned one of their projects at Pozières for a more ambitious project to blow up the belfry of Our Lady.

Quietly placing his pistol next to the rifle, he was about to purloin the regimental dispatch messenger peered cautiously past the wire beyond the trench. Ernst standing in the shadows behind this surly *schütze*, tapped him on the shoulder and politely inquired, "*Cigaretten?*"

In breach of German military discipline, the soldier relinquished his rifle to receive a cigarette. At that moment, the Regimental Dispatch Messenger grabbing the rifle disappeared over the top of the German trench, leaving the soldier to explain to his sergeant how his Mauser had morphed into a Luger.

Sprinting several bounds unseen, the *gefreiter* heard a guttural whisper calling him in. A whisper he could have ignored but chose to heed. A whisper, which caused him to change directions, trip and fall head-first into an enemy-occupied shell-hole, driving his rifle muzzle-first into the mud. A decision, which may not have been entirely volitional since the comfort of hearing a German voice in No Man's Land to lone German solider was as if a whisper from Wagner had instinctively directed the *gefreiter* towards the comfort of a German-occupied shell-hole.

The agony of a heavy object smashing into his scrotum was met first with a sense of betrayal and then an overwhelming wave of excruciating pain. Struggling up his assailant's legs, the *gefreiter* desperately grasped at this traitor's throat, uttering guttural curses until his helmet was torn from him; the strap jerking back his head, the helmet crashing down upon his skull.

When the *gefreiter* regained consciousness, he found his hands grasping his injured groin and two menacing Australian's bearing down upon him. One of the Australian's forced him to release his grip; whereupon a further wave of agony sent him back into a state of unconsciousness.

When he again awoke, shivering, he discovered he was staring directly into the piercing eyes of a young Australian with an ardent desire to shoot him in the face. The second Australian was now on his stomach observing the German trench system from the edge of the shell-hole.

The *gefreiter* stopped shivering and silently glared back, fighting and fortifying himself against his suffering. Flares were fired from both the Australian and German trenches but were noticed only in as much as the flickering light and the waxing moon illuminated the determined Australian's face.

He began to ignore rifle fire and rounds whizzing over the shell-hole. The sickly-sweet smell of his own blood and fresh dirt exposing the decomposing flesh of the dead disappeared. His sense of touch and taste diminished and both soldiers' struggles shrank to a steadfast stare.

Oblivious to the passage of time, the *gefreiter* stared outwards towards the object of his derision and inwards into the depths of his mind. He simultaneously caught fragments and glimpses of future hopes and memories. He hoped Ernst would deliver his message and return to Regimental Headquarters. Ernst could then feed little Fuchsl, his dog. But these hopes becoming inconsequential soon drifted away.

Upon focusing even more intently upon these fierce young eyes, the angry features of the surrounding face began to blur; reducing the *gefreiter's* fear of being shot. Ultimately, his fear of death began to dilute to a mere indifference. In the intermittent darkness, his face softened and he perceived in the dull black eyes glaring back at him, fleeting reflections of himself; as the moon displaced the shadows beneath the Australian's Brodie helmet, at once revealing a momentary glint.

The *gefreiter's* self-examination superseded his glare at the Australian, who had injured him. The deeper into his mind he delved, the more his physical agony abated and his memories and hopes disappeared into insignificance. Eventually, time suspended at five minutes to seven on the church clock of a vaguely impressionistic watercolour the *gefreiter* had painted as a boy; where he remained until

93

disturbed by the gentle touch of a hand on his shoulder and the whispered words, "This too shall pass."

**

Later, whilst under urgent treatment at Regimental Headquarters, little Fuchsl nervously appeared, jumped around a bit and barked before being bundled-up and tossed outside. The yapping of the little terrier outside was restorative to his master. Heavily medicated, the anticipation of Fuchsl slobbering over him, running in circles and snuggling up to him at night reinvigorated him to recover.

Thoughts and reminiscences began to flood back into the *gefreiter's* mind. At one moment, he imagined he threw a small red ball and little Fuchsl would fetch and return it, waiting for it to be thrown again. At another moment, he imagined he could feel little Fuchsl licking his hand and dancing around his feet. The sensation although somewhat repugnant, elicited a slight censure to this unruly little creature but as an act of subservience between a dog and his master it was also quite pleasant to the *gefreiter*.

The *gefreiter* remembered when he and Fuchsl were celebrating with friends, Ernst, Fritz and Hans: eating, drinking and laughing together, well away from the front; enjoying the warm summer breeze on their faces. A warm symphony of flowering black-eyed Susan sprinkled amongst the long grass, stimulating the senses: the sun further reddening already ruddy faces.

"Who ate all the sausages?" quipped Ignaz.

Fingers pointed at poor little Fuchsl and they all erupted in laughter.

In his haze, the *gefreiter* realised that the simplest moments of acceptance by a few friends would ultimately outweigh the disingenuous accolades of the masses. Eventually, the theft of this loyal little dog would cause him the deepest despair. But even then, this too shall pass. The *gefreiter* had unconsciously learnt a lesson of indifference: conferring emotion excessively upon one sentient being created apathy towards the suffering of the many.

With the *gefreiter's* trousers removed, the Turkish surgeon inspected the improvised dressing upon the wounded scrotum. Immensely interested in the innovative Australian medical procedure, he was unaware of the adhesive properties of the tape. Slowly tearing the tape from the scrotum, the surgeon inadvertently aggravated an already weeping wound.

The *gefreiter's* eyes immediately opened wide and he let out a piercing shriek. Causing the surgeon to spring back in surprise, the remaining tape was torn from the scrotum exposing a solitary testicle. The *gefreiter's* cries were drowned out by barking little Fuchsl outside, realising his master was awake and wanting to play a game of fetch the ball.

***

"Where is 3848 Lachlan Watts?" Peering from behind his curtain, Berenger gruffly asked Albert Watts. Albert had baptised Berenger's blanket the Turin Shroud; a black joke, which had permeated 10 Battalion Headquarters, whilst Berenger slept.

"Sir," Watts stood to attention, heels together, eyes at 45 degrees above the parallel, affording the coincidence not to come into contact with Berenger's glare.

"In the absence of one of the Battalion Dispatch Messengers, who failed to return last night...um. He was seconded as a replacement."

"Upon whose authority?" Berenger angrily enquired.

"Last night after you left, a senior officer came in to 10 Battalion Headquarters. He said our telephone communication lines were being cut by artillery fire and that we needed more Battalion Dispatch Messengers, one from each company..."

"How did 3848 Watts come to be selected as a battalion runner?" Berenger emphasised the words 'battalion runner', knowing that the selection process was not based upon aptitude or experience.

"Sir, I don't know, sir," blubbed Albert Watts upon realising the significant risk his brother was now facing.

"You are aware 3848 Watts was trained as a Company Storeman, not a Battalion Despatch Messenger, are you not?" Berenger cross-examined his corporal.

"Sir, yes, sir," Albert Watts bit his lip to stop it from quivering.

"You did not explain in defence of Private Lachlan Watts, that his skill-set was required here rather than as a Battalion Despatch Messenger, which requires a rifleman's skill-set?"

"Sir, no, sir."

"You did not offer advice that training a new supplier in logistics would be less efficient than rotating Battalion Despatch Messengers from the infantry platoons."

"Sir, no, sir," Albert Watts head slumped somewhat.

"Chin up, Watts," came the gravelly censure.

"You did not ask for documentation as to the authority for this senior officer to make such a decision?"

"Sir, no, sir,"

"Who was this officer?"

"Lieutenant Colonel de Wett, sir."

Watts espied in the half-light Berenger's face turn a shade of red and then purple. He heard Berenger's teeth grind. Berenger, upon discerning that Watts could sense his rising anger, turned his back but Watts could see Berenger's hands curling tightly into fists.

Composing himself, Berenger turned back and with a resigned smile said, "Thank you, Corporal Watts, stand-easy. I suggest you will be even busier in the next few days organising your stores. I authorise your pending request for assistance from the platoon sergeants to assemble their own stores' requests with you in the absence of a trained supplier."

"Allow me to make you a coffee and we'll plan for this contingency."

Albert Watts returned a relieved smile in exchange for a wink and said, "Sir", which meant, "Yes."

The remaining 10 Battalion company commanders and assorted officers began to descend into the crypt and congregate around the large map table that occupied the centre. Presently, the Regimental Sergeant Major drew everyone's attention and the hushed murmurs became deathly silent.

The Commanding Officer appearing from behind a curtain fashioned from a blanket akin to Berenger's (but unlike Berenger's blanket, as yet unbaptised) shuffled some papers upon the map-table, nodded to an anxious-looking major with glasses and said, "Intelligence."

"Sir," the Major deferentially nodded in reply.

"Sunrise will be at 6:06," he said authoritatively.

"First light is at 05:46," Berenger muttered, correcting two concepts of the intelligence officer's first sentence: 1) first light is more helpful to the soldiers than sunrise, and 2) the 24-hour clock had not yet come into use in the Australian army. Berenger, (who had learnt the 24-hour clock in the war in South Africa), ensured that all three Watts' boys knew it to avoid the obvious confusion that may occur in relying on a system, in which the time repeated itself twice each day.

Berenger waited for the next two pieces of slightly less than helpful information. "Sunset will be 8:44." On more than one occasion had matters scheduled for 6:00 in the morning commenced at 6:00 in the evening: with obvious disastrous results.

The Major's brief contained some egregious inaccuracies stemming from what he had heard from the brigade rather than the recent observations that Berenger had reported earlier in the day.

"Brigade advises that our artillery has breached the enemy wire."

The Commanding Officer's eyes focused on Berenger, who, ever so slightly shook his head. Berenger received a small but appreciable nod in response. The Intelligence Officer's speculative briefing did little to assist the Commanding Officer's orders for the Fighting 10th South Australian infantry battalion to commence an assault upon Pozières the following morning. Berenger was unsurprised that the catastrophic number of casualties at Fromelles would be supplanted by further catastrophic casualties at Pozières.

He raised his chin slightly, acknowledging to the Commanding Officer that he was aware of the inevitable immediate future of the *Fighting 10th*. The Commanding Officer nodded slightly to his company commanders after his orders, which was correctly inferred as gratitude for loyalty and service. Ultimately, through his furrowed brow and craggy face, the company commanders knew it was unlikely they would encounter either him or each other again.

Before disappearing into the night to return to their companies, Captain Hemple spoke to his Acting Company Sergeant Major.

"Sergeant Bekker will take up the position of organising the wounded after the advance tomorrow. We will need you to take over from Bekker, when we reach Pozières as he will be required by his platoon. Also, the Commanding Officer authorises Private Lachlan Watts to return to the Q store, but to date, I understand he is dispatching messages to the companies. When he returns to Battalion Headquarters, he can remain with you and signals to re-establish field-telephone communications with the forward trenches."

Berenger listened intently to his acting company commander.

"Sir," he replied to the second half of Captain Hemple's instructions without committing himself to the first.

Berenger had determined that if the barbed wire had not been displaced, neither had the Germans behind it. He believed that wherever the *Fighting 10th* were unable to make any further progress, they may be better positioned to go to ground and sap, knee-deep closer to the enemy trenches.

The saps could be used to resupply ammunition and trenches could be constructed at advantageous positions to sight Australian machine guns for counter-machine-gun fire. However, first Berenger had to brief the company quartermaster and signalmen as to their possible responsibilities. If field communications were to be laid behind the advancing troops the signalmen would be permitted to traverse the sap carrying ammunition for the riflemen occupying and extending it. Otherwise, he would invite them to take an alternative route and "go over the top". The cynical smile appeared as he climbed the stone-stairs to find the battalion signals' sergeant major.

***

As the *gefreiter's* shrieks and tears subsided, he was left sobbing and whimpering on a stretcher to be relocated from the Medical Transit Station to a Field Hospital. Two over-worked orderlies placed the stretcher outside beside other injured soldiers awaiting transport.

Only securing the *gefreiter's* injured scrotum with a few delicately placed sutures to prevent any further immediate damage before inspection at the hospital, the surgeon had run out of anaesthetic.

Unlike the other wounded soldiers, who lay stoically on their backs on the ground the *gefreiter* adopted the foetal position with his hands between his legs and army blanket drawn up over his head. The blanket did not deter Fuchsl as he was so happy when he sniffed out the *gefreiter*, he jumped for joy all over him.

Trying to pull the blanket off from covering his head, little Fuchsl barked and growled at his master, very much enjoying the game of avoiding a weak hand trying to throttle him. The scene brought great joy to the injured soldiers, some of whom could have aggravated their injuries had they continued laughing so hard.

Gerhardt the ambulance driver arrived after narrowly avoiding another Australian artillery bombardment. His little ambulance tottered and spluttered between craters and potholes to finally come to rest in front of the wounded soldiers.

Gerhardt was an affable and good-intentioned, slightly portly German lad with glasses. He was a qualified medic with quixotic ideals well above his medical skills. Unfortunately, his lofty ambitions of trying to save the Imperial German Army by tending to the sick and injured were never realised. Patients, who were transported from the Medical Transit Station often arrived at the Field Hospital in far worse physical condition solely due to Gerhardt's kind and well-meaning administrations.

Meanwhile, Fuchsl had worked his way under the *gefreiter's* blanket and was tussling with an ever more frustrated and angry patient cursing and thrashing about beneath. Unaware that the patient was being assaulted by his little dog, Gerhardt approached the stretcher to investigate the happenings beneath the blanket. He nodded benignly to the soldiers, who were now in fits of laughter, which caused Gerhardt to respond with a perfunctory smile. He maintained his genuine expression of care and concern as he knelt down and cautiously began to lift a corner of the blanket.

Fuchsl who believed the *gefreiter* was hiding the small red ball in one of his hands held firmly between his legs, sniffed around and barked at the *gefreiter*, playfully biting into his crotch, whilst narrowly missing a punch from an angry fist. Finally, in a fit of rage the *gefreiter* yelled at the playful little dog, "*Fuchsl aus!*"

Gerhardt, who understood both English and German, misunderstood that he was the unwarranted victim of a vulgar English slight; and that the soldiers, some of whom had now rolled off their stretchers were laughing at him. Maintaining more than the modicum of control expected when faced with such embarrassment, Gerhardt decorously placed the corner of the blanket down, pouted, stood up, and waddled back to his ambulance.

The two orderlies rushed over to remove little Fuchsl from beneath the blanket and momentarily secured him in the Medical Transit Station, relocating the spitting and groaning *gefreiter* in the foetal position on his stretcher with the cover over his head to at least confer a final vestige of dignity to this suffering German soldier.

Unknown to Gerhardt, who was in the process of conducting a seven-point turn to reorientate the ambulance with the rear, facing the stretchers so that they could be loaded more efficiently, the *gefreiter's* stretcher had been placed on the road to be loaded first. When Gerhardt ran over the *gefreiter's* foot, he realised that the guttural sounds of German invectives, which followed were now actually directed at him.

The orderlies harried by little Fuchsl, barking and dancing around their feet, who had now escaped the Medical Transit Station rushed to bundle-up the stretchers and load them on the ambulance. The whistle and the inevitable explosion of Australian artillery shells was the signal for Gerhardt to go.

Without securing the ambulance door or the *gefreiter's* stretcher the ambulance took off. Bumping and jostling the hapless patients within, Gerhardt wound his little ambulance around pot-holes trying to avoid being blown-up. Before the ambulance disappeared from view, in the middle of the bombardment, the rear doors of the ambulance flew open and the *gefreiter* fell out. The last the orderlies saw was brave little Fuchsl playfully running to his master to play yet another game of fetch the ball.

8. The Calm Before the Storm

Vater unser im Himmel,
geheiligt werde dein Name;
dein Reich komme;
dein Wille geschehe,
wie im Himmel so auf Erden.

The Lord's Prayer

Private Lachlan Watts had been delivering messages between 10 Battalion headquarters located in Our Lady and front-line Australian trenches, where small work parties of soldiers were attempting to cleave their way through the German wire at Pozières before sunrise.

In the absence of confirmation that the wire had been breached, Lieutenant Colonel P-W had presciently instructed the company commanders to ensure they had cleared at least one clear path through the wire per platoon. He required updated reports before midnight so that he knew where company commanders would re-site their machine guns in the event, they found suitably advantageous ground.

However, those soldiers who volunteered for this task had no training in achieving it; and in their over-enthusiasm, a work-party of two were illuminated by search-light and shot dead by rifle-fire inspiring the Germans to focus an arc of fire from one of their machine-guns upon a soldier from Hindmarsh; ignominiously spread-eagled upon the barbed wire, intestines exposed.

Private Lachlan Watts was now in a predicament. Fixed in No Man's Land by the periphery of the search-light that had spotted the soldiers attempting to cut through the wire. He could no longer traverse his intended route back to the lines of the *Fighting 10th* as it was now illuminated all the way back to the Australian trenches.

Lachlan Watts decided to slither, parallel to the German trench until securely out of the gaze of the search-light and make-up on lost time by sprinting back in one bound to 10 Battalion lines in the dark. However, he had not counted on crawling across ground held by the 9th Queensland infantry battalion, who were quietly preparing for their assault.

From classical Athens and before, they who held the extreme right-of-line had earnt this honour by their reputation in battle. Other battalions would claim, the 9th gained the extreme right-of-line through a twist of numerical fate. But tomorrow was Queenland's day. Tomorrow, Private L would rise from the parapet and wreak vengeance with his bayonet as his comrades fell dead beside him. With every mate that fell, the more desperately he drove his bayonet home until all that remained was his will to keep going. But for now, Private L was on sentry at the company machine-gun post.

One of the sentries spied movement coming in from the flank. As no soldiers had left through the machine-gun position, the Queenslander logically calculated that the movement was German.

Lachlan Watts sighed in relief in a shell-hole when after a moment's pause he determined that he had crawled to relative safety. Sweat trickled down his brow as his breath slowed and he regained composure: safe.

Watts realised his message would be delivered late. He believed that if he zig-zagged the remaining distance in the dark, he could return to the Australian trenches. He could cover the open ground in a single bound and relay the information to the company commander that the wire had not been breached.

Like the German dispatch messengers, Watts did not carry a rifle because he was able to move faster without one. But unlike the German dispatch messengers there was no pistol for him to carry, so he dispatched his messages unarmed.

Watts crouched like a tiger on all fours, before rising out of the shell-hole with every ounce of speed he could muster. Exhilaration at avoiding being shot by the Germans turned to astonishment when a flare ascended into the night sky, exploded at its apex, illuminating Watts as he ran even more wildly towards the Australian lines. The Australian round that lodged in his leg sent him screaming into another shell-hole.

"Gotcha, you German bastard," came the muffled words from the Queensland trench.

Lachlan Watts curled into the foetal position hugging his right leg, biting his lip in the hope that he was not seen going to ground by the Germans, who had trained another search-light across the shell-hole in which he took refuge.

"Are you ok, chum?" a feeble voice, followed by a tentative pat from the bottom of the shell-hole.

"Of course, I'm not bloody ok," Watts emitted an angry whisper.

"I've been shot in the leg."

"Let me help you, chum," said the voice, feebly from the dark.

"Where are you from? I can't tell from your voice," Watts enquired through a wince.

"I'm a runner from the British 48th Division: Ox and Bucks, that's me," he said apologetically.

Watts could not see this boy's face at the bottom of the shell-hole, but he sounded young. The boy carefully lowered Watts into the dark; Watts cursing like a sergeant.

"Keep your hand on the wound, chum. I will keep you safe from shrapnel."

With that, the brave little British soldier covered Watts' curled-up body with his own.

"I have to say, chum. I'm lost. I've come from across Bapaume Road to deliver a message to the 3rd Australian infantry brigade. I ran behind your brigade and I thought I'd take a shortcut back, but I did not realise your battalions are not lined up. I've run into No Man's Land, and now I'm stuck and I can't move," he said rather unconvincingly.

Watts had other extremely painful problems presently on his mind. He'd put his finger inside his wound to stem the blood. He was determined to stick it out until he was rescued, so he bit his lip to remain quiet. He was grateful that he shared the shell-hole with another soldier, albeit in a compromising position.

A German sniper had relocated to take advantage of any movement caught within the scope of the search-light and whilst searching the ground to his front identified not Private Watts, but a potential location for an Australian machine-gun.

The Queenslander, who had shot Watts did not allow Private L to fire as it would have given away the machine-gun's position to the Germans. He exposed his head above the parapet to which, the silhouette of his Brodie helmet became an attractive target. The German sniper round, which struck him in the face caused brain detritus to splatter upon the now dumb-struck Private L. The dead body slid silently to the bottom of the trench to rest against a slumbering soldier, who'd slept restlessly through the shooting; now contently sleeping against a warm corpse.

In a mere moment, a flare had illuminated Lachlan Watts dashing towards the Australian lines. As no patrols had recently left from the 9th Battalion positions an Australian sentry shot and wounded him. The rifle fire and Watts' unintended scream drew the attention of a German searchlight, which in turn illuminated the sentry, who was killed. The round fired by the German sniper at the Australian sentry entered his face, lodged in his brain and extinguished his life – all in the calm before the storm.

***

Meanwhile, Berenger was arguing with the 10 Battalion signals' sergeant major.

"Who gave you authority to order my men to carry ammunition?"

The question was posed to Berenger like a rhetorical statement, in which the first word would have been, "Nobody."

"Sir, I invite *your* men to carry ammunition if they want to use any sap created by the infantry tomorrow, otherwise *our* men will be required to resupply themselves and *your* signallers will get in their way. Therefore, I invite *your* men to go over the top in the alternative," Berenger caustically responded.

The signals sergeant major puffed out his chest. Acting Company Sergeant Major Berenger becoming frustrated curled his fists but turned around and stormed back to Battalion Headquarters in the hope that Lachlan Watts had returned.

At 4:30 a.m. hot breakfasts arrived within the sand-bagged entrance of Our Lady, where the sergeants and several lance corporals had congregated to take breakfast back to their troops.

All the lance corporals were asleep; even the ones who were standing up, leaning against the sandbags. However, Sergeant Bekker had reported that the last time he saw Lachlan Watts was when he reported the dispositions of two successful breaches in the German wire.

Sergeant Bekker had advised his platoon commander that this would become a defile that the Germans would focus their fire upon. He had notified his platoon commander, who had already requested one of the company machine guns for covering fire for the morning of 23 July 1916.

Bekker suggested the point at which the platoon commander had requested the wire-cutting party to remain all night would become the forward point from which, casualties could be extracted and water and ammunition could be more effectively supplied.

"Good work, Bekker," Berenger nodded.

Bekker beamed like the private soldier, who for the first time in his career was called by his name and rank by a superior without a preceding expletive.

***

"Fifteen minutes, Sergeant Bekker," Captain Hemple whispered as he looked at his watch.

"Sir, that is, Acting Sergeant Major Berenger, sir," Berenger politely corrected Captain Hemple by placing 'sir' at both ends of the sentence.

Captain Hemple shot a surprised look at Berenger, which was received calmly. Hemple turned his head to look towards the enemy trenches and smiled in such a way that Berenger could not see him.

Berenger had sent Bekker back to his platoon and taken up his rightful place as Company Sergeant Major. Beside him stood: Albert Watts, two signallers armed with telephone cable and two medics armed with a stretcher. He had dispersed the other signalmen and medics to the platoon sergeants, who advised that Berenger held only these four men in reserve and after that, there was no more.

Bekker's platoon commander instructed his corporals to find depressions in the ground, shell-scrapes, and cover by constantly observing changes in the terrain to their front. They instructed their corporals to update their sketches of the paths they were taking so that every pair of soldiers knew exactly the route they would take and the numbers of bounds they would make until finally they reached the wire.

At the wire, the corporals had determined that a whole section would go through with the fire support of the other two sections. The final section would break into the trench with the fire support of the two sections, who had gone to ground through the wire.

With 10 minutes left until zero hour, Berenger called the sergeants into him.

"Allow the corporal of the first section to arrive at the wire to consider this option: first section through the wire, straight into the trench. Whilst the second section goes through the wire, the third section provides fire support. Any questions…Go!"

In the trenches of the 9th Queensland infantry battalion, similar last-minute preparations were taking place.

"Jack, it's me, mate. Make room, I'm going over the top with you," said a burly private to his old schoolmate as he tried to step up to the parapet.

"How about you go over the top when you're bloody told to," growled his sergeant, yanking him down.

"I'm sorry, sergeant."

"Don't be bloody sorry. You can be bloody sorry, when you bloody take, bloody Pozières," he growled again.

This time with a wink and a pat on the soldier's back.

The Queenslander ground his teeth. "Right. I'm gonna bloody take, bloody Pozières," he said to himself.

But the sergeant had already gone down the line and was dressing down another soldier.

The 11th Western Australian infantry battalion, reinforced by a company from the 12th Tasmanian infantry battalion had been bickering with each other about everything including spurious inter-company allegations that their sisters and their mothers were the same people.

At nine minutes to zero hour, some of the 11th overheard the Tasmanian company commander whisper within earshot, "Remember Lieutenant Colonel C. Do this for him, boys."

The 12th battalion commander had raised the battalion within three weeks as one of the first of the Australian Imperial Force. He trained them and trained with them. He suffered with them and occasionally laughed with them, every day until shortly after 4:30 a.m. on the 25th of April 1915, when at Gallipoli, Lieutenant Colonel C was killed.

"For Lieutenant Colonel C!" the whisper was repeated through the company, through choked-up voices.

The battalions of the famous Australian 1st infantry brigade: famous to date partially because of New Zealand-born, Captain Alfred S. and Australian-born Lieutenant Leonard K. had fought their way into Lone Pine. Once they were there, they weren't going to give it back: two more Victoria Crosses for Australia.

This they felt more than any hour hitherto was Australia's hour. The revelation that 5 Australian Division had lost 5,513 casualties in 24 hours at Fromelles would not have been known to all the Australians facing their fate at Pozières. But what would have ground through the rumour mill percolating down to the lieutenants and second lieutenants, the lance corporals and privates standing at the parapet with less than eight minutes remaining of their mortality was that at Fromelles, Australian casualties were catastrophic.

Despite this realisation, several days later thrust into the breach the Australians would doggedly fight on. Unlike at Fromelles, Australian soldiers at Pozières would not be fighting for Britain. Australian soldiers would be fighting for Australia.

The soldiers of the 1st Australian infantry brigade were no longer last-year's long-dead ex-public schoolboys of Sydney's elite but were joined by hardened miners from Broken Hill, New South Wales. With broken teeth and broken noses, who in the next seven minutes would fight like devils and die for Australia; leaving broken promises, broken dreams, and broken-hearted loved ones to cry unrequited tears.

Sweethearts, who would grow to womanhood, dotage and death, whose last remaining memory of these brave young men would be a touch of a hand, a fleeting kiss at the wharf, a tearful eye and a last anxious embrace. Pining for a sweetheart from the moment he disappeared into the bowels of a troop-ship and finally, tears falling upon a snapped streamer, clutched tightly in a delicate hand.

A woman's hand, which over the years and decades would perhaps have worn the wedding ring of another; and becoming worn with care, have raised children to adulthood. Becoming wrinkled with age, withered hands would have dandled grandchildren on aged, wrinkled knees; and a living heart, which did not forget the image of tears falling upon a streamer clutched in a once delicate, smooth hand.

A human hand, which could in the end still curl into a fist, fingernails piercing old dry skin; no longer clutching the streamer but revealing the sadness and anger of a broken heart within. The streamer, the last vestige of a connection with a fiancé destined never to return.

Reminded every ANZAC day henceforth, that their sweethearts would probably have been part of the low-life and dregs that previously littered the streets of Sydney, Melbourne, Brisbane, Perth, Hobart, and Adelaide. The remembrance consistently re-opening wounds that were never allowed to heal.

At the very end even the long, deep burning sadness that had pervaded the private moments of their lives, the memory of a delicate young hand, desperately clutching the snapped streamer, tears streaming, fingernails cutting into flesh would eventually disappear into insignificance with their passing.

Battalion upon battalion of Australians and British packed filled trenches facing Pozières: a palpable crescendo of tension, grinding teeth, grumbling soldiers, surly looks, shoulder-to-shoulder, sweat-stained tunics, rifles, fixed-bayonets, glinting under enemy flares; six minutes to zero hour.

The Germans were ready, and the Germans were confident. Had they not repelled the British in five previous assaults upon Pozières? Had not hard lessons been learnt by the deaths of their comrades? Let them come on again. Let them. Let them feel the scythe of death. Let their mothers weep. Let us bleed Australia dry. We shall not retreat.

The Germans had been intercepting signals since La Boissel. The two lifeless South Australians hanging on the old barbed wire had confirmed a pending attack and had given the game away. Despite Berenger's best efforts the *Fighting 10th* now faced the most determined defenders in the sector, reinforced by fresh German battalions currently standing in reserve trenches. Wire, which had been cleared in the evening had been repaired pre-dawn and machine guns accordingly re-sited.

To the catholic Bavarians, weary of the persistent patronising of the protestant Prussians this would be their hour. Let all the children of Munich and Nuremberg read aloud the names of the dead. Let mothers weep for their departed souls; bodies buried anonymously in an unknown grave reserved only for a pitiful *poilu*.

"Five centimetres right, Fritz," the machine-gun corporal re-staked the right arc of the machine-gun to cover those paths in the wire intentionally left unrepaired to allow the Australians to permeate in the defile.

"Ja, ja," came the frustrated answer of the soldier, lifting the heavy machine-gun again for the fourth time in as many minutes. The soldier, whose second summer away from his father's farm; his brothers' dead and his parents ageing, in different circumstances could be forgiven for his faltering concentration. The filthy look which, met his answer was accordingly responded to with uncomplaining compliance.

Clips of ammunition were stacked neatly just below the German parapet to save German soldiers the time of delving into their ammunition pouches to reload. The moon exposed rifles protruding rudely from loop-holes between sandbags on the parapet: five minutes to zero hour.

The underground explosion to the front of Berenger's trench instantaneously killed almost all those in his proximity. German aerial reconnaissance had confirmed the pending assault. The ambitions of the German tunnellers to undermine and blow up the belfry of Our Lady was supplanted by more urgent concerns.

Explosives had been silently shifted into the tunnel overnight and detonated under Berenger's trench to disrupt the Australians. All those on the footstep at the parapet including the new company commander Captain Jack Hemple were blown into oblivion. Berenger and Albert Watts, standing in the trench were swallowed up by the ground as if devoured by a giant subterranean beast.

The shock waves penetrated the surrounding companies of the *Fighting 10th*; disorientating minds and disfiguring faces. The explosion was by no means large but it was effective: 4 minutes remaining until zero hour.

9. Singh

His Majesty the KING has been graciously pleased to approve of the grant of the Victoria Cross to the undermentioned man for his conspicuous acts of bravery and devotion to duty whilst serving with the Expeditionary Force:

For most conspicuous bravery on 10th March 1915, at Neuve Chapelle. During our attack on the German position, he was one of a bayonet party with bombs who entered their main trench and was the first man to go round each traverse, driving back the enemy until they were eventually forced to surrender. He was killed during this engagement.

London Gazette

More than a million valiant men volunteered from the sub-continent for a war which was not of their making; for causes, many of the humble could not have understood and for many reasons foreign in origin. Romantic ideals were rapidly erased with the onset of a European winter. Catalysed by saturated uniforms slowly turning to ice on frozen backs; searing cold, biting into frozen bodies, the temperature plummeted during the bitter winter of 1914. Cold numbing the quick, teeth chattering in a sodden trench; Indian soldiers consoled by a common condition, sharing weak tepid tea with comrades suffering a similar malaise or worse.

Indian intellectuals gambled that involvement in a European conflagration could catalyse Indian independence. They could sense the scale of European social upheaval. The metamorphosis of Europe could precipitate far-reaching effects for India. It was for Indian politicians, leaders and intellectuals to compel the British that through the gains and sacrifice of the Indian army that those effects would be politically positive for India. But soon, very soon, all too soon after the hostilities ceased the expectation reduced to hope and the hope dissolved into a dream.

The establishment of a middle school in Karanprayag, Uttarakhand was measured against the slaughter of Sikhs in Amritsar in 1919. Disappointment was manifest in the parsimonious attention to public memorials of remembrance and the absence of commemoration of brave men and their loved ones, who suffered through the Great War for Britain not for India.

Slaughtered in their thousands, tens of thousands, loyal to the death: gallant Gurkhas and Gharwalis, dogged Dogras, proud Pathans and Punjabis left beloved India never to return. Men of faith: Muslims, Hindus, Parsees, Sikhs, men of their word; enlisted, served, fought and died in battle. Many, true to their faith refused the British Brodie helmet proudly wearing the turban of their tradition, now blood-stained, mud-splattered and dead.

The fields surrounding Neuve Chapelle were littered with the detritus of brave men, who died far from home; fighting to their last breath. Men, who would never see their families again, lay silent and anonymous: forgotten. A duplicate Victoria Cross worn on the sari of a teenaged wife, left alone to tend her dead husband's livestock, until she too, lonely and weary with age passed into oblivion to all but a few.

***

Berenger was swallowed up by the earth as was Albert Watts, the two stretcher-bearers, the two signalmen and many of those proximate to their company commander. Captain Hemple was dead. His body had disintegrated in the explosion. He ceased to exist. The stretcher bearers' bodies and the signalmen would be recovered only to be relocated and reinterred with many other men, who in the next four minutes would die in the assault on the German trenches at Pozières.

Albert Watts was screaming in agony; both legs broken. Berenger had been engulfed into the earth. He was unconscious but alive and like many of the others, buried. In Berenger's mind he had remained at the parapet until zero hour, when he clambered out of his trench with the *Fighting 10th*.

He ran directly towards the enemy along his preordained route, slipping through the Australian wire without obstruction, running without effort, breathing easily. Berenger felt a warm wind at his back urging him on. A deep wine-red haze emanated from the horizon, soothing his senses but for a persistent buzzing oscillating in his ears.

When he arrived at the German position, he found it had been abandoned. The gentle wind followed him into the trench and dislodged a fragment of a map from the footstep and blew it in apparently random directions around a corner and out of Berenger's view. With rifle at the ready, Berenger patrolled cautiously anti-clockwise around the trench until it appeared he had returned to approximately the place where he had dropped down onto the footstep. The map lay fluttering before him on the abandoned duckboards.

Strangely, no other South Australians had as yet made it into the trench and neither had he found any Germans therein. He called to Captain Hemple, "S-i-i-i-i-r!"

But no sound came from his mouth. He tried again, "S-i-i-i-i-r!"

Nothing. And again. "S-i-i-i-i-r!"

Berenger became anxious. His calls emitted no sound. There was only a continuous buzzing in his ears, which would not abate. He decided to move through the trench in the opposite direction; this time a little less carefully. But soon enough he found his way back to the map fluttering on the ground.

"We have the trench," he mumbled to himself.

"I must inform battalion that we have the trench. Watts, where are you? Wa-a-a-a-tts!"

Nothing. Berenger sat on the footstep of the fire-bay considering what to do next. His rifle lay across his knees. He bent forward to examine both ends of the trench, which disappeared abruptly at traverses, obscuring his view. He discovered no movement in either direction, only a swirl of air and dust.

Suddenly, a disconcerting figure appeared. Berenger, jumping up with his rifle pointed directly at the swarthy little soldier and shouted aggressively, "Halt!"

The approaching figure stopped, nodded and calmly smiled in acquiescence. He was wearing the British uniform. He was an Indian soldier wearing a British uniform.

"Get down on your knees!" Berenger ordered.

The soldier complied and got down onto his knees, palms exposed in obeisance. His expression remained placid; his face, serene. Berenger detected a soulful yearning in this man's eyes; an expression incongruous to an infantry assault on an enemy trench.

His haunting expression was devoid of anger or hatred. Big kind eyes waited patiently whilst Berenger squinting, summed up the present situation.

"Do you speak English?"

"Yes, sir," the man smiled.

"You are going to stand up and walk around the trench. I will follow you. If you try to run away. I will shoot you. Do you understand?"

"Yes, yes sir," he grinned obsequiously.

The soldier rose calmly to his feet and began to walk slowly around the trench. After a third inspection, in which Berenger peered cautiously into every bolt-hole and bunker but did not ascertain any changes or any sign of life. He said curtly to the soldier, "Sit down."

The soldier attempted to sit on the footstep.

"No, sit on the ground," Berenger growled.

The soldier calmly complied at sat cross-legged on the ground.

"What are you doing here?"

"I'm going home," said the soldier calmly.

"Home? Where is home?" Berenger interrogated him.

"I live in Uttarakhand near Nanda Devi. Nanda Devi is the Bliss-giving Goddess. The most majestic mountain in India."

"You are not entitled to go home," Berenger looked haughtily at the soldier sitting cross-legged and gently gesticulating with his right hand.

Berenger noticed a deep wine-red ribbon protruding from the closed hand.

"What do you have in your hand?" he pointed with the bayonet of his rifle.

"It is my Victoria Cross, sir."

"Your Victoria Cross?" said Berenger, unconvinced.

"My Victoria Cross. I am taking it home to give to my wife, Sergeant Major Berenger."

Perturbed that this soldier knew his name, Berenger believed that if he allowed the soldier to continue to speak, he would regain the initiative.

"Sergeant Major Berenger, sir. I want to tell you about the Kurukshetra war in our great epic, the Mahabharata. Specifically, I want to tell you about Prince Arjuna and Lord Krishna. Before the great battle between the Pāndava brothers and their cousins the Kauravas, Prince Arjuna identifies members of his family, friends and his dear teacher, Drona aligned against him.

The recognition that he must fight and kill those, whom he had hitherto loved undermines his motivation for battle. But dharma dictates that Arjuna must fight irrespective of his desires to refrain from doing so.

Was not Arjuna a warrior? Had not Arjuna trained to fight? Had not Arjuna determined his fate by the myriad of decisions he had previously made during his life? Had not

Arjuna all but made his decision to fight, even before the question was asked?"

The soldier wiped his brow with his sleeve.

"I tell you, sir, I did not want to leave my wife to fend for herself. I did not want to leave India. But I chose to be a soldier and I, all but chose to serve Britain despite many valid arguments against Indian independence, even if I did so. I fought at Neuve Chapelle. If we Indians had not arrived the Germans may have fought their way to the sea and the British may have may not have been able to hold the line. I do not know how this would affect India. The British have recognised my service by awarding me the Victoria Cross. I, myself do not think I am worthy of such a decoration as many of my friends braver than I, fought and died unacknowledged.

In the end, I fought for my friends. I did not fight for Britain. I did not fight for India. I fought for my friends. I fought my very best because it was my duty to fight. It was dharma. But now I am going home, sir."

The soldier's words had a profound effect on Berenger. He did not answer. But relaxed his weapon and beckoned to the soldier to pass through. Berenger knew that had not all four battalions of the brave Indian Garwhal brigade attacked, the von Schlieffen plan may have succeeded and the Germans would have won the war.

Berenger also knew that the Garwhal brigade had suffered greatly for little immediate tactical effect. Out of sincere respect to this brave little man, Berenger lowered his rifle and bowed his head as arose and departed.

When the soldier had disappeared behind the traverse, Berenger sat on the footstep and attempted to devise a plan of what to do next. He began to feel dizzy and he reached for his water bottle. The cool fluid assisted in regaining some of his senses as it trickled down his throat. He felt his breathing becoming difficult and he felt that he was going to pass out.

He lay panting on the footstep, now starting to fight for his breath. Then as suddenly as before, the Indian soldier appeared from behind the same traverse from which he had appeared previously. It was as if he had merely walked and continued to walk around and around the trench; and that he had been walking around the same trench for over a year, indicating to Berenger that he would never return to India.

Berenger now felt helpless. His breathing was very short indeed and he felt the Indian soldier's hands loosen the collar of his tunic. But the kind measures were too late. Berenger had fallen into unconsciousness.

Welsh whispers permeated Berenger's mind as he inhaled a draft of stale life-preserving air.

"This one's okay," whispered the Welsh accent.

Berenger now knew that he was still alive, but he did not consider his condition to be 'okay'.

The explosion had not only engulfed the men near Captain Hemple but had exposed a British shaft dug by Welsh miners below the German tunnel. Berenger had passed through the German tunnel into a deeper subterranean level occupied by the British intent on mining to Pozières.

In his dazed state, Berenger realised that the Indian soldier had been a manifestation of his mind of which, he did not immediately realise the significance.

"He is alive." The Welshman peered carefully at his charge before dragging him by the shoulders, supine along the narrow-cramped passage.

Welsh miners pressed themselves flat against the low wall to allow Berenger to be dragged through. A larger space carved out of the chalk acted as both a make-shift mortuary and a medical treatment facility. Awaiting Berenger was Edith, now dressed in her nurse's uniform, crouching low wearing a benign but concerned expression.

When Berenger was lain supine on the cold chalk, Edith began her survey of his injuries. She carefully ran her fingers through his short hair and held them up to the lamp-light to check for blood. Gently talking to him, she whispered, "Where are you injured, William?"

Berenger did not answer. Edith checked the back of his neck and again held her hands up to the lamp-light: nothing yet.

"Talk to me, William. Tell me where you are injured."

"My head, Edith. My ears are ringing," Berenger feebly replied.

Edith observed some clear fluid dribble out of an ear and coagulate on the chalk.

"Where else, William? Keep talking to me," she surgically hovered her candle above his face. Berenger fixated on the flame flickering to and fro, thought about the lives that had been so arbitrarily extinguished that he wondered why he had survived.

Somewhat foolishly, he started to give an account of the Indian soldier. Words that would usually have been transcribed for medical purposes; words, which would have been recorded to complete a mental health dossier that would have tended to show that Berenger's war was likely to be over. But in this instance, no such transcription was recorded.

****

The explosion caused immense consternation in the trenches of the *Fighting 10th*. The 10th and 12th infantry battalions were centred between all four of the battalions of the 1st Australian infantry brigade to their left and the 11th Western Australian and 9th Queensland infantry battalions of the 3rd Australian infantry brigade to their right. Fortunately for the *Fighting 10th*, they were dug in slightly back from the battalions situated on either side of them.

In their urgency, the Germans had uncharacteristically miscalculated and set-off their explosion short of the South Australian entrenched positions. In relation to casualties caused in the Somme campaign they were so negligible as not to warrant even a sentence in an English newspaper. In terms of casualties at Pozières, the numbers were insignificant but would be duly recorded for posterity; etched in stone – in France.

But the mother of two brothers, ex-alumni of Blumberg Primary School, Adelaide Hills would cry bitterly when she read the unfortunate news in the *Advertiser*. Her grief-stricken, usually stoic husband would try to console his inconsolable wife until he could find some privacy of his own, in a far corner of his under-worked farm. His son's sheepdog, Argus sensed the sadness of his master's elderly father; licking the tears from a creased inconsolable face and weathered hands.

Through his grief, the old man expressed, "It's okay, Argus. We've got a lot of work to do today, old boy."

Argus looked solemnly into the old man's eyes and sensed his master would not return. Argus could not easily express his sorrow to the old man, but the old man knew he was also grieving. Argus would work today as he had never worked before. He realised that the old man would soon die and there would be nobody left to look after the farm or the old man's wife. The old man's wife would be forced to sell the farm at a reduced rate and move to Adelaide, where she would find sewing and domestic work until she too, passed away in a society metamorphosed by grief.

Argus did work very hard. As the sun rose, Argus and the old man set about working on the farm without rest until sundown. There was an emptiness in Argus' heart, that no matter how hard he worked he was unable to unburden it. He ran and puffed and panted with his tongue hanging out until there was no saliva left. But still, he could not dislodge the burden. Argus' powerful heart pumped blood through strong sleek legs, oblivious to the effects of hyperthermia draining his body; his mind willing himself to complete this Sisyphean day.

He licked the old man's hand again when he was told, "You did good today, Argus," and was chained to his kennel, weakly lapping from a bowl of water.

With a gentle pat on his head, the old man said, "I'll see you tomorrow."

But Argus would not see the old man tomorrow. Argus had worked hard all day, in his sorrow refusing water until now. His bones ached as he lay down exhausted. Argus had given everything. He knew his master was dead. It was too late for his kidneys. When Argus closed his eyes, he dreamed of his master. He dreamed of when he was a puppy and his master was a boy. After school, his master would come home from Blumberg Primary School and they would play a game.

Argus' heart stopped beating and he died during the night. In his mind, he had snuggled up to his master in front of the fire listening to the gramophone, master stroking his ears.

10. Private Reginald Atkins: The Ox and Bucks

Here rests his head upon the lap of Earth
A youth to Fortune and to Fame unknown.
Fair Science frown'd not on his humble birth,
And Melancholy mark'd him for her own.

Elegy Written in a Country Churchyard

Thomas Grey

During the assault on Pozières, Private Lachlan Watts would lay wounded, breathing lightly in a crater with the British despatch messenger protecting him from German shrapnel with his body. This drew some haughty glances from advancing Queenslanders, who happened to cross his path. Most were more presently concerned with hacking into the Germans than what one Queenslander unkindly referred to as, 'two star-crossed lovers locked in an embrace, hiding in a hole,' as a witness for the prosecution at hapless Private Atkin's trial for cowardice.

The generally facetious evidence was meant for the 10th South Australian battalion despatch messenger, who had gotten himself shot in the thigh to boot.

"His own stupid fault," the Queenslander unnecessarily added.

Although the Queenslander had never mentioned cowardice, his braggadocio was intended as inter-battalion banter between the *Fighting 9th* and the *Fighting 10th*. However, by delivering such an inflated and unintentionally spurious account, he had contributed to inadvertently condemning this British soldier of the Oxfordshire and Buckinghamshire light infantry battalion to death.

Private Atkins had indeed been sent from the British 48th Division to deliver a message to the Australian 3rd infantry brigade headquarters. An Australian 3rd brigade staff officer gave evidence that the message was promptly delivered. He compared the time that Private Atkins received it to the time that Private Atkins had delivered it; emphasising that this 18-year-old dispatch messenger crossing Bapaume Road subject to withering German fire was as fast and efficient as any Australian battalion dispatch messenger on the Western Front to date.

The British prosecutor, an Oxford University trained barrister, who had never stepped foot within Cowley Barracks, Oxfordshire shrewdly pointed out that Private Atkins ran behind the Australian entrenchments to 3rd Australian infantry brigade headquarters, which was not the most direct route. The most direct route from 48th Division was to cross Bapaume Road between the Australian 1st infantry brigade and the German positions.

"Sir," the British prosecutor pronounced accusatorily to the Australian 3rd Brigade staff officer.

"Your evidence is complete hyperbole. I offer to this court the circuitous route that Private Atkins took *behind* the

Australian lines to despatch his message as evidence of his cowardice."

The barrister took a deep breath and offered a censorious look at Atkins, one of the two prisoners.

"Private Atkins was found on his return journey, uninjured, hiding in a shell-hole on the Australian side of the road refusing to move either forward or back. I suggest your comparison is not only erroneous…but fabricated."

The Australian looked at the British prosecutor, mouth agape and his face went a deep shade of red.

"No further questions of this witness, Your Honour."

The extremely embarrassed staff officer left the stand, red-faced but possessed the courage to look directly into the eyes of Private Atkins and Private Watts. Tears welled up in Atkins' eyes and rolled down his face, as he nodded in gratitude to this colonial officer, who hung his head and slumped his shoulders when he returned to his seat to think that he could not have done any better.

"I now call Lieutenant Colonel de Wet," the British prosecutor pronounced stentoriously. De Wet pompously entered the court, took the stand and swore his oath. By the time he took his seat, his eyes had met the stare of Private Watts' Commanding Officer. At that moment de Wet decided to slide a little further down in his chair and speak in a softer voice than he had originally intended.

By the time he had completed answering preliminary questions as to his name and rank it had become obvious to de Wett that he had incurred the wrath of every 10th battalion officer present.

"Lieutenant Colonel de Wet," the prosecutor led him in dulcet tones.

"Would you be so kind as to tell the court how Private Watts came to be a battalion despatch messenger?"

"Watts volunteered," de Wet lied.

"Why did he volunteer?"

De Wett started looking around the improvised courtroom as if trying to find an equally improvised answer.

"He wanted to get out of the attack on Pozières," he lied again.

The 10th Battalion Regimental Sergeant Major coughed, stood up and excused himself from the court-martial.

Berenger as acting counsel for Watts deferentially rose to his feet. The prosecutor hearing the slight scrape of Berenger's chair turned to see defence counsel rise, bowed slightly and took his seat.

"Mr Berenger," said the presiding judge.

"With respect your Honour, Lieutenant Colonel de Wett is unable to look into the mind of Private Watts as to why he became a battalion despatch messenger; and even if Private Watts said the words that Lieutenant Colonel de Wet alleges, the Court may only consider the words for the fact that they were said, not for the reason why Private Watts became a despatch messenger."

"Mr Parkinson, do you have a response?"

"Yes, your Honour, I do," Mr Parkinson rose to his feet.

Mr Berenger sat down.

"I accept Mr Berenger's assertion that Private Watts' words may only be considered for the fact that they were said, not for the assertion that the words were true. I respectfully add Private Watts' words accompanied Private Watts' actions. I submit that the timing of his acceptance is when he learned his battalion was to attack the German positions, not when he learned the position of battalion messenger was available…"

"Your Honour, that was at precisely the same time…" Berenger interjected, jumping to his feet.

"Sit down, Mr Berenger. One more outburst like that and I'll hold you in contempt."

"Your Honour." Berenger used the words, 'Your Honour' in the same non-deferential way that he used, 'Sir', meaning neither 'yes' nor 'no'.

"Mr Parkinson, please continue."

"Private Watts was found at the far right of the 3rd brigade line. He had escaped…"

"Mr Parkinson, shall we use the words, 'he had traversed?'" His Honour suggested a more neutral verb.

"Private Watts had traversed completely beyond the front of the 11th battalion trenches and was traversing through the front held by the 9th battalion, beyond which he would have escaped the assault," Mr Parkinson explained, using the word, 'escaped' again in a sentence. This time, Mr Parkinson conveyed a future tense but not dissimilar to the sense for which His Honour had censured him for.

"Mr Berenger," His Honour said.

"I will answer the objection, which you are entitled to make," His Honour looked at Berenger.

"Mr Parkinson, Private Watts was found beyond the 9th Queensland battalion trenches. However, I am as yet not persuaded that he intended to escape the brigade attack unless you have an evidential foundation for it."

"Your Honour, Private Watts need only to have returned less than 100 yards to the 10th South Australian battalion positions. Yet he chose to *traverse* at right angles more than

300 yards almost to the end of brigade positions in the opposite direction to the Oxfordshire and Buckinghamshire Battalion, from whence there would be no attack.

Had he equally *traversed* at right angles in the other direction, he would have had cover from the four battalions of the 1st Australian infantry brigade; had he crossed Bapaume Road he would have had cover from the 48th Division.

Private Watts has elected not to give any evidence at his trial. I respectfully invite the Court in absence of evidence to the contrary to infer that the direction of Private Watts' *traverse* was intentional; and that his intention was to avoid battle. To put it plainly, a coward is a coward is a coward," he finished sanctimoniously.

"Mr Parkinson, I have warned Mr Berenger about improper interjections. I am now warning you about unsubstantiated speculation. You have laid no evidential foundation that Private Watts and Private Atkins were in collusion as they hitherto did not know of each other's position, moreover each other's existence. You know full well that I am unable to consider your unsubstantiated claims. You must desist."

"No further questions of this witness your Honour," Mr Parkinson bowed and sat down, red-faced.

Seated in the dock next to Private Watts, in his mind Reginald Atkins had become resigned to his fate. The voices were just blurred to him now as he thought about the last year. He had joined the Ox and Bucks as a pal. That word stuck in his throat because all his pals were now dead. Every single pal that had joined from the great estate had been killed and the Ox and Bucks were not even officially classified as a Pals' Battalion.

But like a great stoic philosopher, Reginald Atkins – all five foot three of him, 130 pounds dripping wet in boots and uniform would say that he was proud to have served his country. He had sworn allegiance to England. He swore allegiance to the King.

*****

The 10th battalion Regimental Sergeant Major went to the brigade regimental police, who were guarding a prize catch. Separated from other German prisoners recently snatched by the *Fighting 9th* from No Man's Land was the *Oberstabsfeldwebel* Warrant Officer sniper instructor.

Whilst checking the position of a German sniper team, which had failed to return to the German lines because they were dead the *Oberstabsfeldwebel* found himself captured by a 9th Queensland infantry battalion reconnaissance patrol returning to the Australian lines.

Mr Hoffman found Warrant Officer First Class Mr Benson, Regimental Sergeant Major of the *Fighting 9th* outside the German's cell engrossed in the documentation about his prize captive.

"Mr Benson, sir."

"Good evening, Mr Hoffman," came the gruff reply, knowing full well that Mr Hoffman would request to speak to the prisoner.

"Alex. There is court-martial taking place at the old farmhouse as we speak."

"I am aware of that, Ben."

"One of the South Australians, Private Watts is being charged with desertion," Mr Hoffman continued.

"Watts will not be executed, Ben," Mr Hoffman said confidently.

"You do know that this matter has gone all the way to Prime Minister Hughes, do you not?"

"I did not, Alex."

"Not one drop of Australian blood will be spilt by the firing squad, Alex. Every Australian has *volunteered* to fight for Britain. No Australian will face the firing squad, only to be executed by Britain for an error not of his making. I can assure you of that. Prime Minister Hughes emphatically responded to the proposition with one word, 'No'."

Mr Benson had as yet failed to persuade Mr Hoffman. Despite Mr Hoffman's restraint, Mr Benson could see a sense of anxiety manifest itself on Mr Hoffman's face. Under the lamplight, Mr Hoffman pursed his lips and looked intently at the floor.

"Alex, the *Fighting 9th* commanding officer also said, No," Mr Benson smiled and paused.

"But he used two words."

Mr Hoffman smiled.

"Maybe we should assist Private Atkins. The evidence at trial indicates that Atkins covered Watts' body during the German counter-bombardment. Instead of recognition for bravery, the British want to convict and execute him."

At that moment a door swung open and a tall, refined English Warrant Officer First Class stepped out of the building onto the cobbled pavement, carefully closing the door behind him.

He stood stock straight, sniffed the air and turned to march directly to Warrant Officers' Benson and Hoffman. Two

English escorts stood to attention, rifle in the shoulder as he passed.

"Mr Robinson, may I introduce Mr Hoffman. Mr Robinson is the Regimental Sergeant Major of the Oxfordshire and Buckingham Regiment, 48th Division," Mr Benson said formally.

"Good evening, Mr Robinson," Mr Hoffman extended his hand.

"Call me John," Mr Robinson shook Mr Hoffman's hand.

"John," interrupted Mr Benson,

"Ben is here to speak to the German *Oberstabsfeldwebel*, as well."

"Gentlemen, it would do the Ox and Bucks a great honour, if I may be allowed to interview the German Warrant Officer. We have learnt through British intelligence that the German army has derived a solution to a disease of the mind called 'Shell Shock'."

The two Australians listened intently.

"We understand that German soldiers are rotated out of the field to deal with their medical condition and are almost all are returned in a short time to fight as enthusiastically as ever. We want to know what kind of treatment they receive so we can implement a similar system of treatment for our soldiers. You realise the French army at Verdun is at breaking point."

"We are aware of that Mr Robinson," Mr Hoffman paused.

"I know and I know, you know Private Atkins is no coward. Atkins is a good lad, who has become mentally ill. Atkins served with distinction at Mons. He behaved in the same manner. At Mons, he risked withering machine-gun fire

137

to drag a wounded comrade into a ditch, saving his life." Mr Robinson paused again, took a breath and sighed resignedly, pinching his chin between his thumb and forefinger.

"Private Watts will be released because he was wounded and unable to move. Private Atkins will be executed tomorrow for cowardice. I'm sorry, gentlemen. If we allowed Atkins to be exonerated because he claims he is mentally ill, everyone will claim that they are mentally ill. The Court-Martial is a matter of discipline, not law," Mr Robinson said punctiliously.

To the disbelieving expressions of his Australian comrades, he added, "Unfortunately, on the Western Front to me it appears to me that law is nothing more."

"The trial finished for the day some minutes ago," said Mr Hoffman tactfully changing the subject.

"We are waiting for Sergeant Major Berenger. He speaks German. Oh, here he comes now."

"Sar' major," said Mr Robinson greeting Berenger in the British fashion.

"Good evening, sir." Berenger stood with his feet together, hands by his sides until Mr Robinson stood offering him his hand.

"Pleased to meet you, sir."

The Warrant Officer corps is a hierarchy within a hierarchy. Mr Robinson correctly did not offer Berenger to call him by his first name because Berenger was a Warrant Officer Second Class with acting rank only and Mr Robinson, Mr Hoffman and Mr Benson were all Regimental Sergeant majors, Warrant Officers First Class as was the prisoner.

The prisoner's cell door creaked open. The German *Oberstabsfeldwebel* stood up: six foot three, the same height as the English Warrant Officer, Mr Robinson, two inches taller than both Mr Hoffman and Mr Benson at six foot one and somewhat towering above Berenger, the interpreter at five foot ten.

"Good evening," said Berenger continuing in German.

"Sir, my name is William Berenger. This is Mr Robinson, Mr Benson and Hoffman," introducing the English Warrant Officer first.

Berenger did not offer his hand because the regulations of rank permitted only the three Warrant Officers First Class to shake hands with each other, and because Berenger only acted as interpreter.

"Sir, Mr Robinson has one man on trial for cowardice. This man is sick. He is no coward. The British have diagnosed him with a new mental illness called 'Shell Shock'. But tomorrow he may be executed for cowardice. They know the Germans have a treatment programme for such cases but they do not know how the cases are treated. They are concerned as much for their men as you were for yours when you were captured," Berenger asked politely in German.

The *Oberstabsfeldwebel* paused and frowned: minutes passed. Finally, he said, "Berenger," and continued in English.

"Berenger," he frowned again and sighing at the facial resemblance of the South Australian to the dead German stretcher bearer he recently saw lying lifeless in No Man's Land. The *Oberstabsfeldwebel* had by name, facial similarity and mannerism correctly discerned that these two men were related. He also determined that Berenger did not realise a related cousin of his had recently been killed.

He did not reveal this fact to Berenger as what use could have been made of telling him that he was related to the stretcher-bearer and then reveal that the stretcher-bearer had been killed in the next sentence.

The *Oberstabsfeldwebel* did not want to cause more grief than necessary. He had three sons himself, the eldest not so much younger than Berenger, the youngest still a teenager all fighting for Germany.

"Gentlemen, please sit," the *Oberstabsfeldwebel* pointed to a bench against the wall.

"Since 1914, we found that some soldiers succumbed to battle fatigue sooner than others, but eventually almost everyone would succumb to what you have termed 'Shell Shock'. German battalions are rotated out of the field in the same fashion as British battalions. But we evacuate a sick man under the advice of the regimental medical officer to the reserve company at any stage that the men are on the front line.

The worst cases are returned for an extended period back to Germany where they are given labouring work until they recover. They are treated like our seriously injured in such a way as to give them the best and most efficient manner of recovery.

They tend to work very hard doing farm labour and tending to crops and livestock because they know their comrades are fighting for them on the front. They are respected for the value of their labour. Those, who retire to the support company may have suffered severe shelling and usually recover after about a day or so. The men, who remain to hold the front-line trenches do not usually mind a replacement because when the sick man returns as he usually returns with food and mail. In this way, we think we retain the greatest amount of soldiers suffering from 'Shell Shock' and preserve morale at home."

The three Warrant Officers stood up, shook hands with the *Oberstabsfeldwebel* and left. Berenger leaving last, bowed and tripped on the doorstep as he stepped through the door; catching himself on the door handle in precisely the same manner of carelessness that the cold dead stretcher-bearer would have done had he returned to the German lines.

The *Oberstabsfeldwebel* smiling to himself hoped he had behaved appropriately and saved soldiers from unnecessary suffering.

11. The Dog That Couldn't Swim

The rich man in his castle,
The poor man at his gate,
God made them high and lowly,
And ordered their estate.

Cecil Frances Alexander
The United Methodist Hymnal, No. 147

The pheasant plummeted from the sky into the lake. James Thomas' favourite golden retriever Jack, marking off the gun instinctively dove into the cold still waters of Leighton Lake on the grand estate swimming through the mist and reeds in search of his master's prey. As the powerful jaws clamped down on the lifeless pheasant a further shot rang out causing the golden retriever to yelp. The dead pheasant released from Jack's powerful jaws floated indolently towards the shore. The wounded retriever, blood pouring from a gaping hole in its face began to struggle; thrashing about in the water.

"Who shot my dog?" 17-year-old, James yelled.

"Who the devil shot my dog?"

The hunting party and gamekeepers all began shouting and arguing with each other.

"Who fired beneath 45 degrees? Come on, own up," James's voice becoming more and more agitated.

James and Arthur Atkins, his keeper ran to the water's edge to see Jack, his retriever slip beneath the surface of the lake.

"Archibald!" James called to his older brother, whom he knew had been shooting with Arthur's son, Reg as his loader. Neither James nor Arthur had learnt to swim. Fourteen-year-old Reginald Atkins, who also had not learnt to swim, ran through the morning mist to where James and Arthur were standing at the lake's edge.

"I'll get 'im, sir," Reg said.

"No, son, it's too dangerous. You can't swim," Arthur tried to catch Reginald's arm, but too late. Reg Atkins dove head-first into the water fully clothed.

The shock of the cold water burnt his face; the cold penetrating his spine through wet clothes. As Reg thrashed around struggling to reach the injured retriever, he felt himself go under. His feet struck the bottom of the lake and he stood up covered in reeds. The water was only about waist deep.

Nobody in the hunting party knew how deep the lake was because nobody in the hunting party had learned to swim and nobody had dared to venture into it. Reg waded out to John's retriever and carefully placed his arms under the body and head.

Slowly moving Jack's wounded body through the water with his head raised so he could breathe through the gaping hole that was previously his muzzle; until Reg, now on his knees, gently guided Jack's body to the muddy shallows where the water quietly lapped the shore.

Arthur thought John had shown remarkable restraint. Although livid with rage, a tear ran down John's face as he crouched down and cradled Jack's head.

"Jack, Jack. There's a good boy, Jack," John whispered, fighting back the tears.

"I've got him, sir," said Reg reassuredly, gently patting him on his upper arm.

"Let's lift him out of the water, sir," he said taking charge.

Arthur had removed his tweed jacket for Jack to lie on.

Reg carefully wrapped the sleeves around Jack's body tying them off to keep him warm.

Jack feebly wagged his tail. His nose and front teeth had been shot-off.

Reg sensed John's anxiety and distress.

"Sir, if we keep him warm. He'll pull through."

Arthur, John and Reg bundled up Jack in Arthur's tweed jacket and by the three of them, they carried him back to the gamekeeper's house.

Mrs Atkin's peered through the kitchen window to see Reg running towards her. He had been sent forward to warn her of the incoming patient. When John and Arthur entered the house with their bundle, Reg arranged a blanket in front of the fire for Jack to warm up.

John lay him down, kissed Jack's ears and started drying him with the blanket. Jack lay very still. He was panting lightly. John discovered that part of Jack's tongue had been shot off. John stood up. He excused himself from Mrs Atkins and walked outside.

Reg and Mrs Atkins dealt with Jack. He would survive but his days as a gun-dog were over. Arthur consoled John, whose grief had turned to anger against his elder brother.

"The spiteful fool," John spat.

"You don't know that, sir," Arthur said. "It may have been accidental."

"It may have been accidental, Arthur...but it wasn't," John replied bitterly, looking at the ground. "Archibald is a proud man. He will inherit the title of baronet. But I am certain, he intentionally shot my dog," said John.

Both John and Arthur turned to see Archibald approaching. Unusually, he was carrying his shotgun over his shoulder. Normally, Reg would have carried it for him, but Reg had run from Archibald to rescue Jack.

As Archibald approached, John and Arthur could see he was not happy.

Archibald stopped in front of Arthur, raised his chin slightly as to be able to look down his aquiline nose at his loader's father.

"Where is your son?" he said stentoriously.

"Reg is tending to Jack inside, sir. Jack has been injured," Arthur said anxiously.

"Archibald, did you shoot my dog?" John questioned Archibald in the manner of an accusation.

"John," Archibald responded in the patronising manner, which indicated he was about to give a lecture.

"My loader grabbed my arm causing the weapon to fire. So, no. I did not shoot your dog," he said somewhat litigiously.

"I cannot believe that," said John dumbfounded.

"I do not care what you believe, John. Ensure your son cleans this weapon would you, Arthur?"

Archibald handed Arthur the shotgun. Without saying anything further or enquiring about Jack. He turned and marched determinedly back along the path, which he had taken to reach the gamekeeper's house.

"Arthur, would you please send Reg out here to me?"

"Sir, I'm sure he meant no harm,"

"Arthur, it is ok. I'm sure Reg meant no harm either," John replied assuring the old man by patting him on the shoulder.

Arthur took the shotgun inside and presently Reg appeared.

"Sir?" Reg asked shamefacedly.

"Archibald said you grabbed his arm causing him to shoot Jack. What do you say?"

"Sir, I did that," Reg looked at the ground.

"You did what? Why did you do that?" John retorted.

"Sir, he pointed the shotgun in the direction of you and my father, sir. If he had fired a shot you could have been hit. We could not see through the mist, sir. We both knew you were standing approximately at the edge of the lake. I grabbed his arm because I thought he was pointing his weapon in a dangerous direction. I am sorry, sir. It was all my fault."

"Reg," John pursed his lips.

"Thank you for your honesty. I do not blame you. You may have saved my life"

"But I caused Jack to get shot," Reg said, his eyes beginning to well up.

"I'm not so sure about that, Reg," John said patting him on the shoulder.

John conducted what could best be construed as a tactile act of compassion by hugging Reg. Reg burst out crying.

"Stop that now, Reg. Go back inside, there's a good man."

***

"Dr Crippen is to go on trial," Archibald exclaimed.

"Archibald, that is not appropriate dinner conversation," admonished his mother, Lady Catherine.

"For murdering his wife," Archibald whispered.

"Archibald, stop," Sir Edward demanded.

"You murdered my dog," said John accusatorily to his elder brother.

"I beg your pardon, John. I'll not have that kind of talk around this table," Sir Edward reprimanded his younger son.

"Father, Jack has been shot in the face," said John.

"Archibald is this true?" Sir Edward asked.

"Father, that fool gamekeeper's boy grabbed my arm," said Archibald defensively.

"Father, Reg said Archibald could have shot Arthur and me through the mist this morning," said John.

"I take umbrage at that. I was there. I know what I am doing with a shotgun and that fool gamekeeper's son grabbed my arm," said Archibald belligerently clenching his fists under the table.

"I will not have this kind of inappropriate argument at dinner," said Sir Edward indicating that he would get to the bottom of the incident in the withdrawing room later in the evening.

***

Sir Edward studied his port as he stood beneath the painting of his father as a young officer in the Ox and Bucks. The roaring fire did little to warm up such a large room.

"Tell me what happened, John," Sir Edward enquired.

"I am the eldest and I was there. Therefore, I should speak first," protested Archibald.

"You should speak when you are spoken to," corrected Sir Edward.

"Reg said Archibald would have fired in my direction. He thought Archibald was handling his weapon recklessly…"

"Why that little…I'll have his hide," Archibald exclaimed.

"Archibald, I have not finished with your brother," said Sir Edward in a more avuncular manner.

"Well, I have finished sir, and I am going to retire," said Archibald.

He finished his port in one swallow discarding the empty glass on the card table for Mr Smith, the butler to retrieve the following morning. Haughtily, Archibald disappeared from the withdrawing room.

The estate had experienced a modest but steady decline in staff since the turn of the century. It appeared that social movements were afoot, whereby in the past Mr Smith had a plethora of applicants for service. Now it appeared that only girls, who had vocational training from the workhouse bothered to apply.

"Asking a scullery maid of 14 to work from 5:00 a.m. to 10:00 p.m. seven days a week is asking quite a lot," said John quite unconvincingly.

"You sound like a suffragette," Sir Edward guffawed.

"If we gave our staff a greater role in the custody of the estate, which we act only as guardians," said John, nodding to the painting of his grandfather, "the servants would discover that they too perform an important role in its preservation."

"Now, you sound like a Fabian," said Sir Edward, unconvinced.

"I am a realist, sir," John said, trying to define his social philosophy.

"Many of the country houses, which expanded in the last hundred years are now in financial turmoil. Father, I fear we may be next and I fear Archibald will be the last Thomas to live in this house. I sense in the last 10 years, since the death of Her Majesty our society has crystallised while the world has moved on."

Sir Edward sighed.

"John, I fear that too. Your grandfather was a small boy at the Great Exhibition of 1851 during Queen Victoria's reign. We had such great hopes then, such inventions for the future: the daguerreotype, the Trophy Telescope, a voting machine…"

"Pay toilets," John interjected.

Sir Edward laughed.

"Yes, pay toilets. I suppose the phrase, 'spend a penny' has been with us for a while now," he smiled.

"My point is John, for whatever faults the Suffragettes or the Fabians say we had, we strived for order, and we strived for discipline. We believed in the inevitable progression of British culture; and for some, social stratification was harder than for others. I am not so naive to say that life in service was a life of equivalence, but at least it was a life."

"There is a verisimilitude between service, serfdom and slavery is there not, sir," John postulated.

"They all start with 'S', John. That is all," said Sir Edward.

John stood up and walked toward the fire. The heat emanating from within causing an already ruddy face to become ruddier. He at least could look at his father eye to eye.

"But now they only want to work in a shop," John began, looking as if he had something else to say.

"You may be right, John. I believe you want to make a suggestion," Sir Edward raised an eyebrow.

"I want to talk about Reg. I know he meant well, sir. Archibald does not like him."

"John, I know Archibald better than you think. I know he blamed Reg for grabbing his arm because I know he would have recklessly fired a shot in your direction. I know he does not take blame easily and I realise his present behaviour will not bode well for the future of our estate."

"Sir, I would ask that Reg learn to drive our Benz automobile. If Archibald continues to drive it, the end of the Thomas name will come sooner than expected," said John, hoping he did not sound too facetious.

"Ah, and you expect Archibald will give him a second chance, if he drives safely," Sir Edward said perspicaciously.

"Yes, I think so," John nodded.

Sir Edward responded with circumspect, "Perhaps you should consult with Arthur first."

***

The victory for John was short-lived. Archibald refused to allow Reg to drive him anywhere but found he helped maintain the vehicle, which Sir Edward considered to be a middle ground.

Soon John, as the second son was commissioned into the Oxfordshire and Buckinghamshire Light Infantry. Whilst Archibald drove the Benz automobile at breakneck speed having consumed copious amounts of alcohol, with Reg dressed in full chauffeur's regalia hanging on for dear life in the back seat.

Shortly thereafter, Sir Edward received a letter from John politely requesting Reg to serve as his batman in the Ox and Bucks.

Sir Edward replied with, "No, meaning No."

He could not afford to lose Reg, (but he may have reconsidered, if John had requested Archibald, given his progressively more uncontrollable behaviour).

Sir Edward respectfully declined a further polite request from the 2nd Oxfordshire and Buckinghamshire battalion commander. Although he thought sarcastically, "Do you want my automobile as well?"

Upon receiving a further polite request from the 5th infantry brigade commander, Sir Edward reluctantly acquiesced and Reg would embark on a new career as a soldier. It was the beginning of 1914 and Sir Edward calculated that both Reg and his youngest son John, now a lieutenant would be home by Christmas.

From 4th August 1914, Sir Edward wore a particularly grave furrow on his brow. Financial straits were beckoning at the estate. Archibald was showing signs of contumacious alcoholism and Sir Edward realised the hope that John and Reg would be home before Christmas was becoming ever more fleeting.

***

On Sunday, Reg sat next to his father, in the socially segregated Anglican chapel on the estate. But not so socially segregated as to prevent Reg from asking Arthur if he would mind exchanging places, so he could get a better view of the rector. In Arthur's mind, originally praising Reg for his interest in the rector's biblical exegesis, he acquiesced to his son's persuasive argument.

Reg could indeed get a better view of the rector by positioning himself at the outside of the row. He could politely peer around the heads and hats of the congregation in front of him to better assimilate the meaning of the sermon.

This afforded Reg the opportunity of a surreptitious sideways glance into the deep brown eyes of Henrietta Stafford, the most junior maid at the estate. Fifteen-year-old Henrietta was young but maintained precocious perspicacity at the import of Reg's gaze. Momentarily capturing both Reginald Atkins' eyes and his heart, she looked away in a disinterested fashion.

The following week, Reg requested that he be able to sit in the same seat. His love-struck gaze was caught by Henrietta, who affected an inclination of her head, and briefly returned the look, accompanied by a coy smile devoid of a blush.

Unfortunately, Henrietta was observed by Arthur, who after the service censured Reginald for his inattentive behaviour, (which he presciently believed to be accompanied by inappropriate thoughts), by asking him what he had understood about Cruden's Concordance.

Arthur was met with an embarrassed expression accompanied by a rambling response as Reg searched for the answers by staring at the sky at the ground and at the sky again. Avoiding eye contact was correctly interpreted as evasive by his father, who advised Reg that, "You will not sit in the aisle seat again."

However, the damage was done. Reginald Atkins had a sweetheart.

***

Reginald went white as a ghost when he was advised of his pending new career in the army. Both Sir Edward and Arthur told him how proud they were of him and that he would be sadly missed. He would be missed more by Henrietta, who was told in passing by the cook, Ms Scran. Ms Scran wondered why Henrietta had lost her appetite at dinner that evening.

"Are you alright, Henrietta? You haven't touched a thing," Ms Scran said with a concerned look on her face.

"I am feeling a little unwell, but I will be okay." Henrietta smiled stoically.

When she finally went to bed, she dreamt she was able to see Reg in his army uniform and perhaps wave goodbye to him as he got on the train. But when Henrietta awoke at 5:00 a.m. she realised that another demanding day lay ahead. She was at least grateful for the dream.

***

Private Reginald Atkins although not the most aggressive of recruits, excelled in training with the Ox and Bucks. His hard work at the grand estate certainly paid off and he learned his trade quickly.

Of significance to his battalion was Reg's almost innate ability to shoot. British Army marksmanship since the Boer War had increased exponentially with the five times as many rounds now supplied to the soldiers in training. Reg incorporated a 'follow-through' method of firing learnt from John and Archibald as he observed them pheasant shooting.

Originally this method was frowned upon by the instructors as they had taught the soldiers to allow the enemy to come into their sights before firing; but when Reg found himself nearly as proficient as some of the corporals, the instructors began to 'turn a blind eye'.

'Turning a blind eye,' if that is what it could be called was significant to the British Expeditionary Force as a paradigmatic shift in military thinking; decisions began to be made at lower levels. The paradigmatic shift even applied to a hitherto military oxymoron; the ability to disobey a lawful command from a superior officer, when the subordinate was in a more proximate position to make a better decision.

The bitter taste of experience against the Boers paid off for the British at Mons. Armed with the Short Magazine Lee Enfield, the German Imperial Army were soon to enjoy a similar learning experience at the hands of the British Expeditionary Force.

When Private Reginald Atkins shot a pheasant flying across the rifle range with a round from his Lee Enfield, the corporals gasped. His sergeant reprimanded him in no uncertain manner for firing at an unauthorised target but unsurprisingly awarded him no punishment. Atkins' platoon commander upon hearing of Atkins' indiscretion warned him that any further antics would be punished severely but reported Atkins' unique style of shooting to his company commander and the Senior Weapons' Instructor.

The Senior Weapons' Instructor, himself a warrant officer feigned a frown upon learning of Atkins' unique method of firing. A method, which he was familiar with but unable to establish as doctrine.

"Sir," the Senior Weapons' Instructor said, with his thumb and forefinger stroking his chin, "would you please send Atkins to me. I will deal him."

He intended to capitalise on the opportunity to incorporate the 'follow through' method of shooting into the shooting programme: well done that man.

"Thank you sir," was Atkins' platoon commander's hurried reply as he turned to leave the Senior Weapons' Instructor's office, neither observing and nor returning the appropriate salute.

To the private soldiers of Atkins' platoon, Atkins was certainly a champion shot. Despite his lack of aggression and empathetic mannerisms not wholly appreciated by his comrades, Atkins received a very desirable commodity: respect.

12. Harriet Stafford

She walks in beauty, like the night
Of cloudless climes and starry skies;
And all that's best of dark and bright
Meet in her aspect and her eyes;
Thus mellowed to that tender light
Which heaven to gaudy day denies.

Lord Byron

Had Harriet's mother survived the illegitimate birth of her daughter in the Sterling Street workhouse, Harriet's life may not have been so arduous. But Miss Stafford did not survive and the arduous path of Harriet's survival ultimately became her own responsibility.

The force of the doctor's hand slapping Harriet's pink buttocks whilst reducing the purple hue in her little face, which had deepened as the first seconds of her young life ticked away, triggered the volitional ability to exercise her little lungs causing her to let out a long, loud and continuous wail.

Cold, antiseptic air entered Harriet's lungs prompting a cycle of screams and sobs until cuddled and calmed by the plump midwife. Little Harriet, although unaware of her less than salubrious surroundings or the marks of shame she would wear throughout her life became aware that she was hungry.

Miss Adelaide, the midwife swaddled little Harriet whilst the lifeless body of her deceased teenage mother was carted off by the doctor's assistant for disposal. Harriet's curious inspection of the pasty, pock-marked face of the plump midwife was overshadowed by the kindly eyes and smiling mouth of a middle-aged woman staring back at her. Accompanied by a gentle rocking in Miss Adelaide's arms, Harriet subconsciously felt safe, causing her to drift off to sleep.

Life in the workhouse was bleak even by the standards of the destitute and homeless as the sun set in the late Victorian Age. Many of the children born at number 1 Sterling Street spent their lives in domestic service only to return from the great houses as the aged, of no further use to their masters to die unloved and forgotten.

Miss Adelaide, herself a child of the workhouse had remained at Sterling Street to devote her life to the care of unwanted babies and orphans. An alternative career path of living by one's wits, which loosely translated in Miss Adelaide's mind as becoming a woman of economical virtues was less appealing to her than raising otherwise unloved children.

Most of the children genuinely loved Miss Adelaide despite her occasional penchant for emotional distance. But even the very young children, who had only recently become aware of their sentience saw through Miss Adelaide's reserve and gratefully accepted her genuine affections when she so infrequently gave it.

Miss Adelaide's plain face, portly appearance and lack of prospects kept her husbandless and bound to the workhouse. Caring for illegitimate children produced its satisfaction for her, which to an extent made up for not having conceived any of her own.

But Miss Adelaide could exhibit a kind countenance towards the children, who called her "mama" as the first verbal expression of a word. Although the babies themselves did not recognise the significance of the sound, Miss Adelaide's kind eyes sometimes streamed with tears of joy as she cradled crying babies to sleep and sick babies back to health.

However, her tears of joy could easily become tears of sorrow and grief as many babies died before reaching the age of one. At least, in their final hours as Miss Adelaide caressed and cuddled them as their little bodies died, desperately ill, they knew that someone loved them.

On Harriet's first birthday, a major milestone for a child of the workhouse, Miss Adelaide bought her a lovely red ribbon. Because Harriet had not yet been blessed with a luxurious head of hair, Miss Adelaide tied it lightly around her forehead and kissed the bow. Harriet gurgled, smiled and said something to Miss Adelaide vaguely reminiscent of 'mama', with a smiling face and bright eyes.

The long and tiring days at the workhouse had just become less tiring for Miss Adelaide and she kissed Harriet's bow one more time. Then rushed to tend to several other fatherless creatures bundled up in their cots, who had woken up and begun their chorus of crying.

Harriet's first years went by without her realising her existence until one day she was able to sit at the big, long breakfast table by herself and abstemiously consume gruel so distasteful that no one at Sterling Street ever considered asking for more.

However, this didn't last too long as Harriet was soon packed off to Leighton Manor where she would learn to work as a scullery maid. Not before Harriet had made Miss Adelaide a posy tied with her prized possession, the ribbon given to her on her first birthday. The accompanying message, "For the next little Harriet, Love H" was received with the big hug, lifting Harriet's little body off the ground and almost squeezing the life out of her.

The words and spelling were taught by Miss Adelaide. But their arrangement and meaning were all Harriet's. Miss Adelaide packed Harriet a little bag consisting of one change of clothes and a sandwich, (which had become all the latest in culinary fashion).

Harriet sat in the coach, all of 12 years old and waved to Miss Adelaide, who fought back her tears. The carriage bounced along the road from Sterling Street into the country where the undulating road wound through fields of green and fields of yellow; where hedges and orderly rows of elm trees demarked and compartmentalised, who owned which plot of land.

Harriet espied a squirrel scamper from a fallow field, under a hedge and in the blink of an eye disappear up and into the leaves and branches of a stately oak tree. The branches reminded Harriet of the welcoming embrace of an avuncular grandfather, which she never had.

Harriet's young musings were abruptly interrupted by the sweaty hand of a middle-aged man dressed in livery touching her knee from directly across from her in the carriage, accompanied by, "Are you going far, miss?" and a salacious gaze.

At that moment the carriage struck a pot-hole causing Harriet's foot to sharply strike the man's shin and he quickly removed the unwelcome hand with a gasp and a wince.

"I'm going to Leighton Manor," said Harriet deflecting her tone downwards at the end of the sentence, thereby ensuring she was not spoken to on their journey again.

The frosty atmosphere in the carriage was one of Harriet's making, turning a potentially dire situation to her advantage. She sat, staring out of the window watching the trees go by until presently Leighton Manor came into view in the distance.

The middle-aged man, whose hand had not so innocently touched her on the knee, sat hands clasped in his lap. He desperately hoped that he would not be reported to his new employers as he was also bound for Leighton Manor. He peered out through the carriage window to view the edifice approaching. To him, it gave the impression of a giant angry face. To Harriet, it was imposing but also gave her the impression of a sense of adventure.

Leighton Manor was not as intimidating as the workhouse and Harriet was excited about writing a letter to Miss Adelaide to say that she had finally arrived.

The middle-aged man disappeared with the butler to become Sir Edwards' valet whilst little Harriet was snatched up by Mrs Scran to learn her trade as a scullery maid. This activity started almost immediately. As soon as Harriet had secured her meagre possessions there was a mountain of scouring pots and dishes, which she attacked without complaint.

By the time she looked up from her labours, two years had passed and she had barely completed any other task. Scouring not only pots and dishes but also the sinks and the scullery floor. Maisie, the junior kitchen-maid had taken up the task of assisting Mrs Scran the cook in the preparation of food such as cleaning vegetables and plucking fowl.

From time to time, Mrs Scran observed Sir Edward's valet looking lasciviously at little Harriet. Mrs Scran effected such a look of disgust that the valet became careful to avoid the scullery at all costs.

Harriet had always been permitted to eat in the kitchen with the cook and the other maids, which caused some resentment from the servants, who ate separately. Thinking that the maids were eating better than them, the valet complained to Mr Smith, the butler.

Mr Smith learned of the valet's predilections from Mrs Scran. Discussing this problem in confidence with Miss Scran, the housekeeper, Mrs Scran's elder sister. Mr Smith had found the valet to be ingratiating, overly obsequious and not entirely honest with Sir Edward.

But he had kept his feelings to himself on account of some of Sir Edward's expensive missing cufflinks. Mr Smith, playing the amateur detective wanted to find enough evidence to remove the valet from service with any house, not only Leighton Manor. What purpose could be sending the valet to another house to continue his proclivities to the bane of another butler, and moreover to another manor?

"Come in, please Miss Scran," said Mr Smith in that way, which reinforced that he both admired and loved her; thinking she would not have known despite never officially stating his position. With 25 years of unsaid signals, Miss Scran knew.

Moreover, although her emotions were better guarded than his, Mr Smith's feelings were reciprocated. It was Mr Smith, who did not realise his affections were reciprocated.

Miss Scran entered Mr Smith's butler's pantry and stood demurely before his large desk waiting to be invited to sit.

"Please," Mr Smith beckoned and moved his hand towards a decanter.

"May I offer you a sherry, Margaret?" he said, sitting behind his desk after Miss Scran sat down.

"Thank you, Mr Smith."

Margaret paused and looked about Mr Smith's pantry. The pantry vaguely resembled the library as Margaret was aware that Mr Smith in pursuit of self-improvement was a voracious reader. She smiled at Mr Smith, which was returned with a smile but could equally have been construed as a blush.

"I know that you are aware of a disturbing and unwanted potential relationship between the valet and Harriet, our scullery maid," Margaret said gravely.

Mr Smith furrowed his brow and acquiesced by nodding.

"I have taken the liberty of enquiring whether Harriet would be of assistance to any other estate. You are aware that she has had an impeccable work record and is a precocious and hard-working 14-year-old."

"Yes," Mr Smith agreed, nodding his head thoughtfully.

"I see a future problem with her…with her…precocity," Miss Scran used the word with some delicacy.

Mr Smith looked at his sherry glass without taking a sip. Placed the glass carefully down and cleared his throat.

"Margaret," he said continuing to use her first name in the realisation that discourse would occasionally reach a more satisfactory conclusion where the participants were on equal terms.

"Mrs Scran reports that Harriet is about to embark on assisting with the preparation of food. Mrs Scran has invested two years into Harriet's development. The role of a scullery maid is often seen as the lowest on our social hierarchy but she has made the best of it. In terms of God's ordering of society that does not mean she is any less of a human being. Little Harriet has conducted herself appropriately, even may I say, enthusiastically with a cheerful disposition. I am loathed to lose her."

"John," Miss Scran said in a soft voice.

"I know Harriet is a good worker but I feel that she may be in some danger. Danger, which becomes more imminent as she matures. I'm sure you would have considered the scandal…"

"Margaret, I'm not looking at problems, which could occur in the next five years. In 25 years Harriet, as you did, could become the housekeeper and we will have played our part in the survival of Leighton Manor."

Mr Smith paused and smiled as if a pleasant memory had entered his mind. "Do you remember 25 years ago when you started at Leighton Manor as a scullery maid yourself as a 15-year-old?"

"You were a footman in those days, John," Miss Scran blushed.

"I was, Margaret," Mr Smith smiled.

Miss Scran omitted the adjective 'handsome', whilst Mr Smith omitted the words, 'I was in love with you'. Yet, even given the relative formality of their surroundings, the words could easily have been interpreted in their glances by a casual bystander.

"My primary concern is for Leighton Manor, Margaret. I will not send Harriet to another house merely because the valet has lecherous designs for her. We must act together to protect the Manor, Sir Edward and Harriet. I shall deal with the valet in such way that he does not find similar employment in any house," Mr Smith said conclusively.

Miss Scran looked somewhat downcast but resigned to Mr Smith's decision placed her hands on his desk to assist her in getting up. The fingertips of her left hand brushed the back of Mr Smith's right hand.

"Margaret, I'm sorry. I should have offered my assistance," said Mr Smith hurriedly as he stood up and made his way around his desk.

"It has been a pleasure to grow up with you, sir. I am looking forward to growing old with you too," Margaret said as she made her way out of the pantry.

Mr Smith, now in his mid-50s at the apogee of his career, also looked forward to a life with Margaret. But first, he had to deal with the valet and even more delicately, deal with Sir Edward.

On Sundays, all would attend Church of England services at the chapel a short distance from the Leighton Manor. It was a refreshing walk conducted at a brisk pace to church where the servants would await Sir Edward and Lady Thomas' arrival by carriage.

Harriet espied an awkwardly handsome and somewhat shy boy maybe a year or two older than her standing with his hands behind his back looking at something in the oak tree. The leafy branches overlooked some of the moss-covered headstones in the country graveyard. Her gaze was distracted by the glint of the shiny black coach of Sir Edward approaching.

In an instant, her eye was further distracted by movement in the oak tree in the direction of the awkward-looking boy's gaze. Then a squirrel ran vertically down the trunk and was about to dart across the path of the carriage when the lightning speed of the hand of a now not so awkward-looking, young boy gathered up the squirrel. In a struggle to contain the frightened creature until the carriage had passed, he released the squirrel to dart-off across the road and under the hedge.

Harriet now saw a brave young man, who could easily have been injured by either the horse or the carriage receive thanks for this selfless act; a scolding from his father and further stern looks from the senior staff of Leighton Manor.

As she sat listening to the sermon and watching the sunlight cause the image of Christ to dance upon the stained-glass windows, Harriet observed through her peripheral vision the furtive glances of the boy peering at her seated in the row across the aisle.

Only ever so slightly, Harriet raised her chin and stared straight ahead affecting an air of aloofness. Reg, lacking the maturity to realise her haughty expression revealed Harriet's interest in him was unable to see the telling sign, from where he was sitting, that a small smile had come upon the right-hand side of her face.

Harriet had innately determined that this young paramour would repeat his gaze the following the week. She even more cheerfully went about at her new labours of preparing food at Leighton Manor trying her best to concentrate on the task at hand rather than the brave young man, over the ensuing days, she had become enamoured with.

On Friday, great consternation erupted at Leighton Manor when it was discovered that the valet and Maisie, the junior kitchen maid had eloped. Miss Scran stood in the doorway of Mr Smith's pantry wringing her hands. Mr Smith stood uncharacteristically with his hands on his hips, deep in thought but angry at the valet. At once he broke the silence.

"You can lead a horse to water, Miss Scran but you can't make it drink."

"This is no time for joking, John," Miss Scran mildly censured him.

"Think of the scandal, if this gets out."

Mr Smith furrowed his brow.

"We have no evidence to be certain of anything, Margaret. But yes, this will not look good for Leighton Manor," he sighed.

"Be careful what you wish for," Miss Scran warned.

"I know, Margaret. I know," Mr Smith touched her elbow as he slid past Miss Parsons to break the bad news to Sir Edward.

***

"What!" Sir Edward replied to Mr Smith.

"If I haven't enough to do already. My son James has accused his brother, Archibald of shooting his dog...and now this."

"May I suggest that I could be of assistance. Miss Scran thinks Maisie may be in the village and the valet may have disappeared independently. I wanted to say that some cufflinks of yours had disappeared but I did not want to spread rumours that could turn out to be false. I suspected the valet but I knew that you thought highly of him and that you would not appreciate my opinion. I am sorry, sir."

"Please, John. Don't apologise. You are right. If you deal with the issue of the valet and Miss Scran deals with the issue of Maisie, I will get to the bottom of James' accusations," Sir Edward said somewhat dogmatically.

"As you please, sir," Mr Smith turned and left, wiping his brow as he excused himself from Sir Edward: imminent disaster temporarily averted.

Sunday arrived and there were no solutions to the problems of the preceding week. The congregation assembled at the little chapel in the usual fashion except for that Reg and his father had exchanged places. This was only noted by a few as their status accorded them seating near the rear. However, it gave Harriet a clear view of handsome Reg through her peripheral vision. His eyes darted around trying to capture a glimpse of her without making eye contact.

Determinedly, Harriet decided to look directly at him. When she had captured his stare and locked eyes momentarily, she lowered her head. She was controlling his love-struck gaze but not his mouth, which due to a loosening of the jaw muscle gaped open slightly. The cheeks went a bright shade of crimson realising he had been found out but upon a very slight smile in return, Reg was able to exhale and return to a certain type of breathing, which would at least allow his lungs to inflate.

However, the beads of sweat that appeared on his brow and beneath the shirt upon his back did not abate even when prompted by an elbow to the ribs by his now disgruntled father.

***

Yet another mountain of pots stacked high in Mrs Scan's scullery. The new 13-year-old scullery maid from Sterling Street stood bewildered amongst the dishes. Harriet having completed her duties as the junior kitchen maid said to Mrs Scran, "I will help you Abbie, I know a few tricks to get through this lot."

"You are a good girl, Harriet," Mrs Scran mumbled as she hurried about some other task.

Harriet observed in this waif of a child before her: uncertainty, loneliness and a lack of any kind of confidence. But a certain ribbon that Abbie wore in a certain knot tied delicately around her blonde ponytail told Harriet that Abbie had been in good hands.

Harriet mused upon Miss Adelaide: her nurse, her teacher and her surrogate mother. She was glad that someone else had inherited her ribbon. She no longer needed it and the gave her a sense of satisfaction that someone else could call Miss Adelaide 'Mama'.

"Roll your sleeves up now," Harriet said as she rolled up her own.

Abbie gasped at the healed scar tissue on Harriet's arms: a healed burn here, a cut there, an abrasion on her elbow and callouses deserved of a fully-grown scullery maid used to labouring with her hands. Abbie had a role model.

"Yes, ma'am," she said as she copied Harriet.

"Ma'am is not for me, Abbie. Please call me Harriet." Harriet smiled at her charge as she got to work. Upon being called by her first name, a sense of confidence came upon Abbie; and a sense of value in her work. Harriet certainly was developing an inspiring way about her.

***

But there were times when even Harriet seemed a little morose; like the time when she found out that Reg was leaving Leighton Manor to join the army and the time she received an official letter saying that he would not be returning.

There were joyful letters too. Reg appeared to be much more eloquent in his written expression than verbally, (especially when trying to talk to Harriet despite the limited chances he had had at Leighton Manor).

Harriet always wrote a carefully worded response, wishing him well and a safe return. She folded Reg's letters in such a way that they were all the same size. Upon pain of death, Harriet would never disclose the one particular letter that would remain forever closest to her heart:

My dearest Harriet,

Just a few lines to say I am well. I trust you are the same. I received your letter yesterday and it gave me great comfort. I am not where I was the last time I wrote, so sometimes your letters take a little longer to arrive.

Harriet, I am nineteen years old next year. I want to tell you something. I wasn't able to say this when we last spoke because I was too shy. But circumstances have allowed me to come out of my shell. When I return, I want to become the game-keeper at Leighton Manor. I know you are doing well too.

Harriet, I want to say, I love you. I have always loved you since the moment I first saw you. I want to ask you to be my wife. I will allow you to consider this and I will ask you again in person when we meet again.

The weather here has been fine and everybody has been in a particularly cheery mood of late.

I am looking forward to seeing you again.

Your sweetheart,
Reg

Harriet looked at her wedding finger, imagining what her pretty although somewhat calloused young hand would look like with a wedding band. With that, she rolled over, pulling the covers up to her cheeks and drifted off to sleep.

13. Maisie Cotton

For such persons do not serve our Lord Christ, but their own appetites, and by smooth talk and flattery they deceive the hearts of the naive.

Romans 16:18

Sir Edward's valet, Mr Walter Crabbe, had intentionally avoided Harriet Stafford at Leighton Manor. It did not diminish his lecherous behaviour towards the remaining junior female staff. The titillation he received from deceiving Mrs Scran, Mr Smith and Sir Edward had emboldened his conduct in private with naive young Maisie, to whom he now redirected his disingenuous compliments.

Maisie was a plain, plump girl, who had muddled through school until age 13. Her parents thought it was time for her to enter the workforce. Although gullible and simple, Maisie worked well in the scullery under the tutelage of the punctilious Miss Scran. Miss Scran, who regarded Maisie as a rough diamond sought promotion for her charge from the scullery to the kitchen. Perhaps, rather fortuitously as the previous junior kitchen-maid had returned to London to work in a haberdasher's shop owned by her uncle.

As Maisie had rarely been complimented by her parents on anything she did as a small child, she became enamoured with the ridiculous accolades lavished on her by Sir Edward's valet, Mr Crabbe. She craved love more than attention and unwittingly acceded. Mr Crabbe even flattered her for how she chopped onions. Although, he had not seen her work but merely smelt her hands whilst committing an act of frottage, conveniently squeezing past her plump figure in a narrow corridor.

Mr Crabbe insidiously cultivated a relationship with Maisie, promising her security and an easier life. He was careful not to be caught with her in a compromising position as that would have meant immediate expulsion from Leighton Manor for both of them. He had learnt from the mistakes that he had made with Harriet Stafford. But he had not learnt to quash his avarice or lechery, but merely to conceal these vices more effectively.

Mr Smith thought Mr Crabbe's answers to simple interrogatives were too polished and too practised to be true.

"Mr Crabbe have you seen Sir Edward's monogrammed silver cuff links?"

"No, Mr Smith, sir. But please allow me to search for them and I will inform you when I do," Mr Crabbe said as he glided out of sight into Sir Edward's library, which he entered only to evade Mr Smith.

Mr Crabbe had surreptitiously devised a plan to persuade Maisie they that should elope without alighting her to the reality that she would be kidnapped. He would whisk Maisie away to London, from whence he had recently relocated to Leighton Manor on account of his less than salubrious associations he had made in the business of importing tea from Hong Kong. His Chinese business associates had threatened to cut off his head and display it on a bollard at the docks because Mr Crabbe had been importing more than just tea.

The Chinese were particularly upset not with what Mr Crabbe had been importing but that he had not informed them of what it was, he was importing. Therefore, by obfuscation Mr Crabbe had not entitled them to their portion of the profits. When a ship was seized in port carrying Chinese tea and Mr Crabbe's contraband, he had acutely discerned his life was in peril. He determined that he would be better positioned to do something else elsewhere. Hence his coach journey to Leighton Manor where he unsuccessfully attempted to ingratiate himself upon Harriet Stafford.

In any event, he intended to permit young Maisie to entertain businessmen in one of the Chinese clubs near the docks as a token of his contrition for failing to inform his business associates of the nature of the cargo they were carrying. Conveniently for him, he had also intentionally failed to inform Maisie of his designs for her.

In the early twentieth century, the importation of opium into Britain was not yet unlawful. Pharmacists controlled regulation causing a growing propensity for the avaricious to proscribe opium illegitimately. Ultimately, this illicit practice gave way to burgeoning British demand from those, who had become addicted.

Demand does not suffer a vacuum for long when a method of supply is achieved. Enter Sifu Ip. After the Opium Wars and the Boxer Rebellion, a crescendo of American and European traders, missionaries, adventurers, many of whom had no business in Chinese affairs, surged into China to expand trade with the Orient. Ironically, capitalism and Christianity coalesced in China to establish an indigenous variety whereby Chinese businessmen, who professed Christianity became slightly more trustworthy with each other than those who did not. This gave Chinese Christian business an edge with both the Occident and Christian Oriental converts.

Sifu Ip professed Confucianism, but his ruthless demeanour towards society in general and business competitors in particular, revealed his purported philosophical beliefs to be a veneer to everyone but himself. For Sifu Ip, Confucian rituals manifested themselves anecdotally in public, but the doctrines were honoured often only in the breach.

Yet Sifu Ip's pragmatic approach to Christianity had a Confucian flavour. He would simply adopt Christianity to ensconce a portion of the Hong Kong supply of opium originating in British India back to England, paying off the ships' masters to leave some of the opium in the hold.

Sinking the unsuspecting British barque, *The Trinity* in the *Fragrant Harbour* sent a menacing message to the non-compliant. The trade conduit, which had opened for the conduct of British business in Hong Kong would create an opportunity for the Chinese to seep like water quietly back into Britain.

***

From the coach, Maisie watched the rolling green fields. Orderly hedgerows interspersed with wild dandelions gradually disappear from rural Oxfordshire. The further

Maisie travelled from Leighton Manor, the less secure she became about her spontaneous decision to elope with Mr Crabbe.

The coach came to a halt. A veritable wave of nausea washed over her as a particularly malodorous portly middle-aged man, reeking of gin and decidedly worse for wear uneasily ascended the step and flopped into the seat opposite Maisie.

An attempt at drunken small-talk with Maisie was met with a glare from Mr Crabbe, whilst Maisie feeling trapped, silently wrapped her shawl ever more tightly around her shoulders. Her head sunk dejectedly as he produced what appeared to be a gin bottle. This man dressed in a thread-bare black morning coat with a bulbous sweating bald head proceeded to tip its contents down his throat and coarsely finished with a large belch to re-establish that Mr Crabbe was not the only alpha male on the coach.

Unfortunately for him, he drifted off to sleep sprawled lengthwise on the carriage seat commencing upon a raucous round of open-mouthed snoring. Mr Crabbe seizing both the opportunity and the sleeping drunkard flung open the coach door and unceremoniously tossed him out. However, not before to Mr Crabbe's surprise, he involuntarily discharged such a putrid gaseous emission as an inadvertent parting shot that Maisie did not know whether to laugh or cry at the sight of Mr Crabbe expelling this drunken churl.

Maisie opted for the former in the immediate reflection of the memory of this man's astonished expression as he disappeared out into the dusk. Eventually, the latter arrived with an unpleasant aroma and she sobbed quietly to herself with her face turned away from Mr Crabbe. Maisie noted that

Mr Crabbe did nothing to comfort her with words or gestures. This made her feel more like a possession than a young woman, who had been slighted. Her intuitions although disconcerting were correct.

Eventually, a gentle rain enveloped the coach. The deep grey clouds intensified the night as darkness fell. Daisy began to feel afraid as though being conveyed into the unseen piqued her consciousness to the dangers of the unknown. Mr Crabbe had drifted off to sleep and Maisie wistfully thought about Harriet and Mrs Scran. In reality, she hoped the coach would turn around and take them back to Leighton Manor. The thought of assisting Mrs Scran in preparing food floated through her mind like fond memories rather than the futility she believed it was whilst she was doing it.

As the coach rounded a bend, Maisie could see a street lamp in the distance. The sight was a welcome beacon giving her a glimmer of hope. Hopes, which were to be dashed when Maisie discovered it was an inn, where Mr Crabbe had reserved only a single room.

Mr Crabbe ascended the stairs with Maisie reluctantly in tow. He unlocked the door to their room, which sounded to Maisie like unlocking a prison cell. Mr Crabbe switched on the recently installed electric light, muted by a stained glass lamp-shade.

Maisie was confronted by a musty chamber decorated with heavy garish wallpaper becoming unstuck and curling at certain places at the juncture between the wall and the chipped plasterwork on the ceiling. Faded heavy drapes enclosed the window to the gilded birdcage into which Maisie was about to hesitatingly enter but stood frozen in the doorway.

The full-length mirror on the mahogany wardrobe reflected a pallid young woman with red eyes but no longer rosy red cheeks juxtaposed with the cadaverous face of Mr Crabbe, the lines on his forehead becoming more wrinkled as if something had agitated him upon entering the inn.

Maisie did not fail to observe that although they now appeared both the same ashen-faced colour that Mr Crabbe's immediate concerns were no longer with her. For the moment, therefore, she felt a little safer.

The green satin bed covering emblazoned with a red Chinese dragon reaffirmed that not only it, but she was out of place in this room. Although she had never before slept in a double bed, she did not relish the idea of sharing it with this strange bedfellow.

Mr Crabbe placed his portmanteau on the floor and waved the key in front of Maisie in quite a menacing fashion.

"You mustn't open the door to anyone else but me. Do you understand, Maisie?" he said without a hint of emotion.

Maisie nodded sullenly. Mr Crabbe turned to leave the room. He did not observe a wry smile extend from the side of Maisie's mouth.

"I will be back shortly. I have some business to attend to," the words drifted off as he descended the stairs. Maisie rushed to the door and quietly closed it. The sound of the key in the lock gave her a moment's reprieve. She would not be opening the door for anybody especially Mr Crabbe.

Whilst considering what to do next, Maisie threw herself fully clothed on the bed and cried. Lying catatonic, she stared at the wardrobe considering it was large enough to conceal a dead body; namely, her own.

"How could I have made such an enormous error?" she said to herself in the way that Mr Smith would have talked to her.

"I just don't know what to do?" were the words that immediately came to mind.

But then a calculated rationale entered her mind. Having noticed a telephone at the desk in the lobby, Maisie decided to ask the attendant to send a message to Mr Smith at Leighton Manor.

Carefully unlocking the door, she peered out before stealing down the stairs. Pausing at the landing, she heard muffled voices but could not hear the words. Had she heard the words, she would not have been able to comprehend them as they were in Cantonese.

At the bottom of the stairs, if Maisie turned left she would encounter the lobby. If she turned right, she would in all likelihood encounter an angry Mr Crabbe. However, Mr Crabbe was not in a present position to express anger. Surrounded on three sides by three inscrutable Chinese gangsters in Western attire, Mr Cabbe's perspiration trickling down his forehead, the uncontrollable shaking of his hands revealed a palpable sense of fear.

Maisie furtively stole a glimpse of this horrid man, back up against a chintz upholstery. Mr Crabbe was facing her but his nervous eyes were preoccupied with whether he was going to be dead or alive in the next five minutes.

A prick of empathy fleetingly entered Maisie's mind, but when the reality of her predicament washed over her, she quickly made her way to the attendant.

"Hello, sir. I would like to send a message to Leighton Manor. Are you able to do that for me?" she inquired in a manner revealing her working life of service.

The revelation bode well for the attendant, who had spent a life in service himself. Discerning Maisie's worried eyes hidden beneath an otherwise anxious expression the attendant shrewdly invited the local constabulary to check the hotel register.

Maisie, scurrying back to her room locked the door and threw herself on the double bed; tears streaming down her face. Although the hotel had recently introduced electric lighting, a candle lay comfortingly in its candlestick next to the bed.

Tears obscuring her view; regrets flooding her mind, Maisie did not see how the moth entered her room, hitherto sealed from the outside world. Absentmindedly, Maisie lit the candle. Its flame gave her at least some comfort, reminding her of Leighton Manor.

The moth, who had instinctively headed for the electric light in the ceiling impulsively changed direction, heading for the candle flame. Almost immediately extinguishing itself upon colliding with the flame, Maisie's expression changed as an insidious idea and a plan of escape entered her head.

14. Resentment

Anger ventilated often hurries toward forgiveness; and concealed often hardens into revenge.

Edward G. Bulwer-Lytton

"They all drowned, you know." Juliana overheard an officious middle-aged woman whisper in a manner to her friend that ensured she was overheard by Miss Fischer.

"Ten New Zealand nurses too. Bless their poor souls." The woman looked disdainfully at Miss Fischer as if she was some kind of monstrous insect.

Astonished, Miss Fischer briefly gasped and then downheartedly looked down at her teacup, her lamington half-eaten, resting on the saucer and her lace gloved hands shaking on her lap.

"The *SS Marquette* torpedoed. They didn't stand a chance. Complete animals, the Hun. Bereft of any civilisation, every single one of them," she uttered in a voice that rudely interrupted the congenial Sunday afternoon conversation in the Glenelg tearooms.

Miss Fischer had wiped an offending crumb from the corner of her mouth but was too embarrassed to raise her eyes to regard her accuser, who had effected a faux English accent.

Gratefully accepting work as a teacher at a Lutheran school to avoid the path to penury, her reception at the tearooms reminded Miss Fischer just how unwelcome she had become in Australia.

Juliana, seven months enceinte glared back at this vulgar woman in couture revealing too much froufrou for these financially straitened times. Catching the import of Juliana's splenetic expression, the woman adjusted her chair so that her back faced Miss Fischer and sensing she was being observed, looked disdainfully through the large front windows.

However, her face exhibiting a flushed crimson, and a droplet of perspiration trickling down her neck from behind her left ear revealed to Juliana that by her outburst, she had merely embarrassed herself.

Leaving their tea and cakes unfinished, the Bäcker family, who had in generations past immigrated from Saxony, stood up, and quietly filed out of the tearooms in an orderly Germanic fashion. A symbol of solidarity with Miss Fischer, which did not go unnoticed by Juliana.

One hundred years ago, before Waterloo, Herr Bäcker's great grandfather had been executed by the Prussians. Subsequently, Generalfeldmarschall Blucher executed a few more, paraded the entire Saxon battalion and burnt their regimental standard in front of them. Australians recognised that Germany had become a state. But the Germans recognised that the state was not homogenous.

"We are going," said Juliana to Miss Fischer grabbing her elbow for support and escorting her through the front door.

The woman and her friend were now in a crowded tearoom surrounded by two empty tables, which nobody dared to occupy.

Juliana immediately felt a pang of indiscretion when she said within earshot, "Miss Fischer we have more to worry about than the snide comments of a spinster." Immediately Juliana realised a sense of suffering in the vitriolic nature of the woman's outburst. Had she exercised greater circumspect, she may have discerned that the name of this woman's son had been recently published in the *Advertiser*; and that this woman was no spinster.

"Miss Fischer, would you please wait for me," Juliana said as they had walked but a short distance from the tearooms.

Juliana returned. As she re-entered, the general hubbub immediately ceased. Juliana walked determinedly to this woman's table where she was greeted with an astonished expression.

"I am sorry for your loss, ma'am," she said quietly.

The woman did not answer. By her expression, the woman had accepted Juliana's apology but the words had cut her very deeply. Juliana bowed slightly, turned and left the tearooms.

Conversation restarted as quickly as when it had stopped. Men continued to discuss horse racing. Some children started laughing when a drink was accidentally spilt. The woman sat mournfully in silence staring blankly out of the tearooms' large shop-front window. Her son's existence and sacrifice had been acknowledged. Eventually, she would forgive the young lady, who had glared at her. But for now, she just sat sorrowfully staring into space.

As Juliana hurried to catch Miss Fischer, she glimpsed from the corner of her eye a recruiting poster in the shop window of the Glenelg drapers for volunteer nurses to serve on the Western Front. Perspiring now, Juliana was mildly censured by Miss Fischer as she waddled along to catch up.

"You shouldn't run so, Mrs Berenger," said Miss Fischer, knowing full well that Juliana would not pay attention to anything Miss Fischer said if she did not agree with it herself.

By the time they had reached Mrs Berenger's home partially by tram, partially by taxi it was just past 6:00 p.m. As 6 o'clock closing had recently been adopted by the public houses, the streets of Adelaide abounded with intoxicated men several times as drunk as they would have been had they been allowed to remain in the pubs a little longer and drink a little slower.

Miss Fischer quickly escorted Mrs Berenger into the safety of her little home where she could rest her swollen ankles. Juliana puffed as she lay on the chaise lounge.

"Miss Fischer, I must volunteer to be a nurse," Juliana uncharacteristically burst out.

"I think not," Miss Fischer said somewhat condescendingly as she slipped into the kitchen to make tea.

"Miss Fischer, we are at war. We all must make sacrifices," Juliana said, sounding more and more like her husband, only less convincing.

"Mrs Berenger, this would indeed be an ill-considered decision," came the response from the kitchen.

"Miss Fischer, I do not mean that I am going this afternoon, but indeed within a year, if I am needed I will volunteer," responded Juliana revealing her decision was a fait accompli.

Miss Fischer paused momentarily, considering that she would be asked to take care of the child, a role that she dearly would have accepted. As a woman in her mid-forties, marriage and child-birth were no longer realistic goals for her.

But fate works in mysterious ways and the warm feeling of the possibility of experiencing motherhood by proxy began to wash over her.

Cool reason entered her mind before she said in a considered fashion, "Yes, Australia needs you, Juliana," using Mrs Berenger's first name.

"Australia recognises the significance of your sacrifice every day because all Australia is suffering on the Home Front. For us, Juliana, there will be no parades, no medals, no streamers and no confetti. Let us be satisfied that we may exist in some certain kind of civilised manner. A civilisation, which although not entirely fair on me because of my German background is a civilisation nevertheless. Let us remain cordial to those, who with harsh words may abuse us. Those, who have lost sons, brothers and husbands for reasons upon scrutiny disappear into meaninglessness."

A moment's silence, whilst Juliana reflected. Presently, but unconvincingly, she answered, "OK."

Reclining on the chaise lounge in a particularly unladylike posture, but understandably given her delicate condition and in the presence of a close female friend, Juliana placed her hands around her swollen tummy and closed her eyes. A sharp kick from the as yet unborn William junior reminded her that the day was not over.

***

William John was born a few weeks prematurely. There was no smack on the cheeks of his bottom when he was born as he screamed and wailed until he was nestled into the arms and breasts of his mother under the proud gaze of Nanny Fischer. The doting nurses gathered around Juliana noting his resemblance to his mother.

When Juliana looked into the enquiring eyes of little William, she could see the eyes of her mother, the eyes of little William's father, and permutations of all those, who went before. The depth of little William's eyes within a mischievous little face evoked memories of herself as a child gazing into the mirror, hoping to be swept up by prince charming.

Cornelia, Juliana's mother had never censured her for such wistful hopes but continued her practical instruction of domestic farm life from baking bread to tethering the horses. The memory evoked the wonderful aroma of freshly baked bread, hot from the oven. The Kruger family, although they never possessed much on the dry South African veldt always held hands around the neatly set dinner table when her father gave thanks and prayed in Afrikaans.

Then the British burnt down her home and took her family to a concentration camp where all but she died of starvation and illness. Cornelia, her mother, Peter Lambertus, her younger brother, Geertje, her younger sister, Magdalena, her youngest sister and Johannes, her youngest brother – all dead.

Pragmatically minded Cornelia realising that she and all her children would eventually die of starvation or disease like many of the other inmates had restricted meagre portions of food allocated to the other children to feed Juliana. Presented with Sophie's Choice, Cornelia gave Juliana a greater chance of survival by ensuring her death and the deaths of her remaining children.

A decision of immense calculation if not mere speculation, which would appear all the colder given Cornelia appeared impassively to watch the lives of her remaining children, Juliana's siblings extinguish one by one until finally, she succumbed herself to sickness, fatigue and ultimately grief.

Even the term 'British' for Juliana, actually meant Australians supervising the concentration camps. The people with whom, she had forgiven and fallen in love with, married, and bore a child in the country she now called home.

Although Juliana's intention to volunteer as a nurse manifest outwardly patriotic motives of sacrifice and duty, deep down, in quiet moments of reflection she acknowledged an overwhelming spirit of adventure and the enjoyable sensation experienced by taking a risk.

Juliana had successfully achieved this before. She had travelled across the world from South Africa to South Australia in the most fleeting of hopes to glimpse the man, she had fallen in love with as a girl. The man, whom she had not seen for more than 10 years; a love, which grew from a hope to an expectation and ultimately a reality.

But also a love, which could be described as a craving, even a dangerous kind of craving. A craving, which if ever satisfied could ultimately prove unsatisfactory. If the man, whom Juliana loved did not live up to the expectations which she had created in her mind, love itself would appear to be a disappointment.

She began to doubt whether the longing for her husband was not merely a justification for self-interest. If William died, who would care for her and her child? How could the efforts of one forthright young woman against the weight of a world at war have any effect at all on the outcome of history?

Surely, she thought all her efforts would be almost negligible.

Almost? At that moment, Juliana despite the impending birth of a child determined that soon, she would volunteer to serve on the Western Front as a nurse.

15. Self-Immolation

Whether 'tis nobler in the mind to suffer
The slings and arrows of outrageous fortune,
Or to take arms against a sea of troubles,
And by opposing end them?

Hamlet

At first, Maisie heard a gentle tapping on the door. Then a disingenuous whisper, "Maisie darling open up." The tapping became discernibly louder and a little more urgent.

"Maisie, wake up darling. Please let me in. Let me in, Maisie."

Maisie froze, catatonic and expressionless, she gazed at the burnt wings and body of the moth, whose life had been extinguished earlier in but an instant. Mesmerised by the flame, her gaze returned to the candle. The flame danced before her, permitting her mind to return to a more pleasant time in her life. A family time, when Maisie regaled to her mother, her father and her two younger brothers a tale of how she single-handedly pulled a calf out of the pond. She had gained the attention and admiration of her family, the people whom, she loved most dearly.

"You will be a stout, strong woman when you grow up Maisie," beamed her corpulent, ruddy father, elbows on the table, broken capillaries decorating his red nose, dripping dribbling down his chin.

Maisie simultaneously beamed and blushed. Her double-chin pronounced as she inclined her head downwards.

"There, there. Good girl, Maisie." Her mother tapping her gently on the back of her pudgy hand.

Maisie's youngest brother pinched her other arm. A warm feeling of acceptance, love and respect washed over her. However humble, Maisie had earned her place in the world.

"Would you like some more dripping, father?" Maisie enquired politely.

"Yes, thank you, Maisie. Surely, you will be a stout, brave woman when you grow up," father repeated confidently.

Maisie knew she was stout as she looked inquisitively at her chubby little hands already calloused from work at Leighton Manor. But brave? No. Maisie did not feel brave.

In fact, as the knocking on the door gradually became louder and the whispers became more menacing, a wave of terror crept up Maisie's spine to enter her mind, catatonically freezing her body.

The whispers had become a growl.

"Maisie, you little bitch! Open up. I know you're in there,"

Maisie did not open up. The growls began to acquire a discernible plaintive character. Maise had won a small but significant victory.

"C'mon love. Open the door," the voice pleaded.

The pleas were genuine. Maisie did not know that Mr Crabbe had been offered a lifeline by his Chinese guests.

189

Either he furnishes Maisie for services at their dockland's *gai dau* (house of ill repute) or he would forfeit his life.

Maisie merely continued to stare at the flickering candle flame. Tears welled up in her eyes as she considered her dwindling options. She felt her young life had become a complete failure. At Leighton Chapel, she had been lectured to on the unpleasant fate of fallen women. Technically, Maisie had not as yet lost her innocence but an unforgiving Edwardian society would judge her harshly. Eloping from Leighton Manor with Mr Crabbe would have created enough impetus for her to fulfil an almost inevitable tragedy.

Unbeknownst to Maisie, the industrialisation of England had precipitated urban drift into the cities and an influx of women and girls looking for work, forced to live by their wits in the world's oldest profession thriving since before Athenian prostitutes flocked to the Piraeus and beyond. Had Maisie known this, she may have been more circumspect in her next course of action.

The tapping on the door had become an increasing crescendo of loud thuds. The sense of desperation was audible in Mr Crabbe's voice.

"Maisie, please. Everything will be alright. Please open the door."

Accidentally or perhaps latently, Maisie knocked the candle over with her foot as she rose from the bed. A cynical smile appearing on her face as she approached the door. Maisie did not realise that the flame had set the curtains alight as she determinedly stood behind the door and said, "Mr Crabbe, kindly leave."

Maisie realised a sense of empowerment as the voice replied from lower down on the other side of the door. Mr Crabbe had dropped to his knees.

"Maisie, darling. Please, what about all our dreams together?" Mr Crabbe pleaded.

Maisie emboldened by Mr Crabbe's plaintive pleas, smelled smoke and looked behind her. The curtains were fully alight and the flames had begun to crackle. She calmly reconsidered her options. Either remain in the room and face her fate or open the door and relent to Mr Crabbe. Maisie's father's predictions were correct. She was both stout and brave. She would remain in the room.

The room quickly filled with smoke causing Maisie to fall to the floor.

"Maisie, open up. Maisie! Maisie!" cried the voice on either side of the door as smoke seeped through into the corridor.

"Damn you to hell then, you bitch!" came the voice and urgent footsteps were heard disappearing down the hall.

Maisie's face affected a serene expression as she drifted into unconsciousness from smoke inhalation. A blessing in disguise as the flames slowly began to lick her clothes. Then quickly her body was alight and soon it was done. But Maisie's consciousness had already returned to her family sitting around the dinner table, her father smiling proudly at her, her mother patting her hand and her little brother pinching her arm.

***

Crabbe quickly made his way down the winding stairs, affecting a faux concern by calling, "Fire, fire, fire!"

The smoke, the flames, the fleeing guests, the converging crowds and the consternation caused were enough to allow Crabbe to slip through both the police and the fire brigade. He threaded his way through the crowd, his head and eyes always looking over his shoulder. Turning into a darkened side street, Crabbe deeply inhaled the stale city air. His perspiration had yet to become cold on his back when a knife belonging to Sifu Ip slipped between his ribs. Sifu Ip fled with a childish giggle leaving Crabbe to bleed out on a dark street.

16. Too Good to Be True

Where do I find such a large frog jumping around the streets?

Cantonese Idiom

The Yum Char restaurant was located on the ground floor of the Ip Building, which opened onto a bustling, narrow Hong Kong street. The Ip Kung Fu school was situated on the fifth floor of the fourth storey; a sanctuary of peace compared to the crowds jostling on the busy street below. The Ip family had intentionally avoided floor and room numbers with the inauspicious Chinese number four, as four sounded like the word for 'death' in Cantonese; not that the meticulous Ip family's propensity for superstition would help them now.

The eldest Ip was known as the Alchemist. The Alchemist was Shyong Huei's father. Shyong Huei was the youngest and only male child of five Ip children. The Alchemist doted on Shyong Huei, allowing his six-year-old son to sit on his lap as he told stories about the Opium Wars on balmy Hong Kong evenings. His girls sat at his feet, innocent, eyes wide and mouths agape with admiration. His wife had heard the stories many times in several permutations before. She became intentionally absent but within earshot, often occupying herself in some small chore preparing chicken for the restaurant for the following day. Shyong Huei didn't have much interest in war stories. He just curled up in his father's lap and completely content that his father and family loved him, fell asleep.

Although the Alchemist had not discovered how to transform lead into gold, he had isolated oestrogen from chicken ovaries. He ground the ovaries with mortar and pestle into a special powder with herbs and spices to stimulate his flock to mature more quickly. Mature more quickly, the flock indeed did.

The Alchemist quietly kept his secret, a secret. The special ingredients were transferred discretely by bicycle to the chicken farmer in the near countryside. The farmer observing the spectacular result, enthusiastically added the special ingredients to feed the chickens. Baby chicks matured to become adults at an alarming rate and were discretely delivered by bicycle from the countryside to the Ip Yum Char dozens at a time.

Almost all parts of the prematurely mature chickens were served sumptuously in the restaurant. Cantonese boys delicately nibbled delicious spicy hot chicken won ton. Old men surreptitiously conducted business over chicken noodles. Crying toddlers' teething was soothed with chicken soup. Voracious and loud hoodlums chewed on chicken feet with great gusto all the while chattering, yelling and arguing with each other; or across from one another at their round tables, or across the restaurant and occasionally even across the street.

Ip Yum Char colloquially became known as 'Chicken, Chicken, Chicken,' a name that instantly brought a smile to the Alchemist and salivation to the hungry crowds, who flocked daily to their favourite restaurant.

The customers had become just so very happy. Ip Yum Char became the most popular restaurant in Kowloon. The Ip family was happy because luck had favoured them with money. The farmer, who sold the chickens to the Ip family was happy because demand had increased, and the farmer was quietly able to increase his prices a little. Luck was with the Ip family, and everyone was happy.

The local Triad thugs, who began to develop breasts as the result of eating the Alchemist's Yum Char special oestrogen-laden chicken were not happy. They were quite unhappy, very embarrassed and extremely angry. Their livid leader Siu Lung Lam, who had developed quite exceptionally large breasts, demanded vengeance on the Ip family after he discovered that the origin of his affliction was the delicious dim sum that he had so voraciously eaten daily for free at Ip Yum Char.

The Triads plotted vengeance deep into the night. Arms folded, feet nervously tapping on the floor, sitting uncomfortably around the Cantonese lantern centred upon a little round table in a cramped room, cluttered with boxes of contraband, discarded objects and general detritus reflecting the frustrated minds of irascible gangsters. The lantern did nothing to ward off evil. In fact, in present circumstances centred amongst the Triads, the lantern invited it. The Triads' eyes glared disconsolately into the flickering flame for fear of catching the embarrassment of another; shadows accentuating rather than concealing their sense of emasculation.

Oestrogen enhanced chicken had exacted a particularly detrimental effect upon Siu Lung Lam's vocal cords. His hitherto menacing voice had risen to a high-pitched falsetto;

more so, when he was angry. The Triads could not hide their laughing eyes behind inscrutable faces when he threatened them. Their reaction (or lack thereof) caused him to become even angrier and his falsetto to become even more pronounced.

Finally, Siu Lung Lam exploded, blaming all around him for his predicament. All garrulously began to accuse each other: pointing, swearing, threatening and shouting.

Siu Lung Lam crashed his fist against the table. The men became silent.

"*Hum ka chan*," (curse the family to death), he demanded in a high-pitched voice.

The Triads nodded and silently left Siu Lung Lam to his rage and humiliation. Alternatively, they could have remained content extorting money from the Alchemist. The Triads could also have remained content extorting money from the farmer, who sold chickens to the Ip family Yum Char restaurant, where they had all eaten for free. They could have remained content extorting all the businesses within their grasp. But as a corollary of avarice, unhappiness inevitably follows in the shadows of a successful enterprise.

No. The Triads must have their retribution. Their anger had clouded their observation that every post-pubescent male, who had eaten Ip's delicious Yum Char chicken had begun to develop unnatural breasts. The embarrassment was shared equally amongst the men in the community contributing to a minor upheaval in the Hong Kong merchant class in a small corner of Kowloon. Muffled giggles by girls at middle-aged businessmen, making their way with their arms folded across their chests were met by glares. But the men continued along the road, scowling with their heads hung low in the realisation that their status had been slighted.

Unlike mainland China, Hong Kong had never fully developed a Confucian scholar class. Confucianism, which had traditionally ordered mainland Chinese society was often honoured only in the breach by some sectors of Hong Kong society. The merchant class had risen spectacularly in wealth, but there was little to ameliorate those, who had opted to forget the salutary discipline of ancient Chinese traditions.

Some no longer worshipped their ancestors. Others had discarded the *chángshān* and taken to wearing European clothing, listening to European music and affecting European manners without realising that the most outrageous and superfluous aspects of European culture and customs merely reflected the crystallisation of Western society on the cusp of upheaval.

But it was others, those not entirely accepted into Hong Kong elites or those not purely Chinese in ethnicity; those, who had European fathers, especially English-speaking fathers that would come to represent a progressive Hong Kong. The marriage of the orient and the occident cemented by the language of commerce that would be continued into the twentieth century at the highest levels by the bilingual sons of Chinese mothers and English fathers.

***

Vengeance in Hong Kong was swift. Shyong Huei was but a block away when he heard shouting from the vicinity of the Yum Char; then screams of women, then nothing. Shyong Huei ran crying back to the Ip restaurant. Fearing the worst, he fought through the crowd that had gathered inquisitively outside the Yum Char. He collapsed to his knees when he saw the body of his father, head hewn almost in two, brains splattered, sprawled across the floor. His sobs turned to howls as he ran about the abandoned restaurant and discovered his mother and five sisters all killed, heads cleaved. No one from outside helped him. No one said anything. No one saw anything. No one did anything. Everyone just stared curiously at the dead Ip family. Such was the fear inspired by the Triads.

Presently, a humble *lou suk ze* (homeless beggar), too old and close to realising his mortality to be concerned about the ramifications of meddling in Triad retribution, tentatively entered the Yum Char. He found Shyong Huei lying on top of his dead father, sobbing inconsolably.

The old man sat next to them. He had a name but everybody cruelly called him Sei Pok Gai in the manner in which loathing and disgust is often imbued with fear, that the vilifiers could eventually become low and cast out upon the street themselves. Having tread carefully amongst broken china, upturned tables, and spilt chicken soup, Sei Pok Gai had inadvertently caused a trickle. Then as the crowd became braver, a crescendo of looters rifling through the restaurant, the kitchen and even the dead bodies of the Ip family to loot anything of value.

The looters avoided Sei Pok Gai because he reeked. Many thought he was crazy. Some thought he was a witch. But with the deftness of a strong, young man, Sei Pok Gai scooped up a dismayed Shyong Huei and carried him in his arms up the stairs to the fourth floor.

Upon entering, Sei Pok Gai lay Shyong Huei against a large sack of rice, into which Shyong Huei pressed his unhappy face, wrapped his little arms as far around as he could and continued to cry. Sei Pok Gai walked cautiously around the fourth floor most of which was open to the sky. He found a pot of red ink and a brush which he took to the door at the entrance of the floor.

In large bold strokes so that the ink ominously dribbled and dripped like blood, Sei Pok Gai painted the Chinese symbol for death on the door of the fourth floor. Then without even bothering to affix the latch, he closed the door.

The cacophony below abated when an angry high-pitched voice could be heard shooing the looters away with falsetto threats. The Triads had come back. Sei Pok Gai gently stroked Shyong Huei's arm softly repeating, "*Yī qiè dōu jiāng guò qù* (this too shall pass)."

The Ip family had organised their building so that the top floor comprised the storeroom and workshop where the Alchemist created his special oestrogen chicken-additive, a spare room with cooking facilities and an open area, in which the Alchemist would teach his daughters and Shyong Huei the rudiments of kung fu, or laundry could dry in the sun. The third floor comprised of a family living space and the second floor comprised of family bed-chambers. The Ip family had indeed been well-off.

The Triads decided to relocate their nefarious opium operation to the Ip building. Siu Lung Lam kept the Yum Char open but customers entered on the pretext of drinking tea but retired upstairs to the third floor to smoke opium.

Sometimes whilst in the arms of Morpheus, they had visions of a little *gweilo* (ghost) darting in and out of the third-floor rooms. But the opium made the addicts initially manifest a kind of indifferent surprise and they would presently return to their stupor; apathetic as to whether the *gweilo* stole their souls. Sometimes, they heard strange noises from the forbidden floor above but again, concern soon drifted off into drug-induced oblivion.

The Triads also heard strange noises from the ceiling of the third floor. Some had even seen the little *gweilo* and heard an ominous growling from above. They said the third floor was for special customers, (meaning opium addicts) but the third floor almost terrified them as much as the forbidden floor which they avoided.

The strange growling was usually Sei Pok Gai sleeping soundly and snoring. Sei Pok Gai would dream of lions with a fish body. Sometimes in his dreams, he would catch one. But Sei Pok Gai did not even own the simplest of fishing boats, so he would be happy hoping that one died of natural causes and drifted to shore before being eaten by a shark.

Sei Pok Gai would usually awake to little Shyong Huei tugging at his shirt wanting something more to eat or a story or just some company. He would always oblige little Shyong Huei as he enjoyed the boy's company himself.

"What are they doing downstairs?" Sei Pok Gai would enquire about Shyong Huei's excursions.

"They are smoking," Shyong Huei replied.

"Sometimes I move very stealthily and creep into their dens whilst they are reclining on their benches. Then I make a great noise and run about the room like a white ghost and then I run away. He...he...he. It gives them a terrible fright. I frighten the gangsters sometimes too. The gangsters don't even like to go to the third floor because they think the fourth floor is haunted. They had to come up once when one of the businessmen died. They had to remove his body. I think opium makes them a lot of money but I think opium is a very bad thing. It destroys people's minds, makes them very lazy. What do you think, Sei Pok Gai?"

Sei Pok Gai nodded.

"Shyong Huei, you are very observant. Opium will destroy Hong Kong. The Triads, who with all their desire wish to make more and more money will only bring themselves down."

"Hmm," thought Shyong Huei.

***

Years had passed. Shyong Huei had become a handsome but immature young man. He never emotionally recovered from the murder of his family. He had unsuccessfully tried to forgive the Triads for their injustice against him but suppression of his feelings only inhibited his emotional development. Shyong Huei dreamed of being a six-year-old boy snuggled up in his father's lap; the centre of attention of his now-dead family. He unknowingly began to affect a childish giggle, which occasionally he would ejaculate even in his sleep.

Sei Pok Gai had grown old and comfortable. The hard times of living on the street had left him. However, fearing those hard times would ineluctably return, he maintained a very simple life. He never left the fourth floor and was happy with his modest yet cluttered surroundings. He watched the stars at night from the open air after eating a little and contentedly drifted off to sleep.

Sei Pok Gai had been a fiery sifu as a younger man. But he had fallen on hard times. He had suffered tuberculosis, which had taken his wife and child. He had lost his business and his home and he had taken to begging on the streets. But even such a baleful existence reaps some small rewards when one searches deeply enough for them.

Sei Pok Gai could always appreciate the warm sea breeze, that whispered gently into his ears that the morning sun would rise on the morrow. He would see the fishermen early in the morning and assist them to unload their catch. He did not ask for anything in return although the fishermen, who were gregarious towards him as they did not seem to notice that he no longer cared for personal hygiene, would although reward him with a small portion of their catch.

Ironically, Sei Pok Gai felt rejuvenated after working so hard. He felt he could stand up straight with his head held high even though he had worked himself to such a state of exhaustion that in reality, he could barely stand up. But the metaphor was enough. Their hands were as rough and calloused as Sei Pok Gai's hands and they respected him for that.

Sei Pok Gai thought a lot about Shyong Huei as he was growing up. Growing up but not maturing. Sei Pok Gai taught Shyong Huei kung fu on the fourth floor. But Shyong Huei would almost always strike the *muk yan jong* (wooden martial arts dummy) after Sei Pok Gai had told him to stop or had told him that his adversary had surrendered.

A late strike or slash would always be administered as a coup d'etat followed by a childish giggle. Sei Pok gai realised that Shyong Huei had not overcome the grief experienced by losing his family but he felt great empathy for Shyong Huei's situation; a despair Sei Pok Gai had experienced himself.

He turned a blind eye to Shyong Huei dressing in his sister's clothes and adorning himself with white make-up before running amok downstairs amongst the opium addicts and the Triads. Dressing as the ghost of his sisters gave him a great sense of empowerment given the fear the Triads exerted over the community.

Shyong Huei always wanted to kill Siu Lung Lam for what he did to his family. However, he never had the chance. But in China, if you wait by the river long enough, the body of your enemy will float by. One evening, Yum Char entertained an opium addict, who was a very wealthy man. Siu Lung Lam was persuaded to ascend to the third floor to extract some clue as to how to extort this man's fortune.

Two of Siu Lung Lam's triads held this stupefied merchant, whilst Siu Lung Lam screamed, threatened and beat him about the head. The falsetto threats were a signal to Shyong Huei to adorn himself in his sister's clothes and administer a thick layer of white make-up.

Shyong Huei did this in such a deliberate and focused fashion that without asking him what he was doing, Sei Pok Gai already knew. He administered each brushstroke with great pressure causing hurt to his face. But Shyong Huei did not feel it. When paint entered Shyong Huei's eyes, he merely affected a slow blink and the tears washed out the paint.

Shyong Huei did not say goodbye to Sei Pok Gai before he left the fourth floor. He pressed the blade into his hand impervious to the gash it made. Brushing past the old man, who did not try to stop him, Shyong Huei's blood dripped steadily as he made his way towards the stairs.

Shyong Huei would avenge his family and he believed he would die today. He deliberately descended the stairs, each step effected in silence. Each step was accompanied by a drop of Shyong Huei's blood as it steadily oozed from him. Fatalism deadened the aching sensation in his fingers as he turned into the darkened hallway. The screaming and sobbing of the hapless addict became louder. Shyong Huei approached the filthy chamber, in which the Triads were beating their stupefied victim. Siu Lung Lam's falsetto voice reached a fevered pitch.

Shyong Huei's breathing became shorter and yet still deliberate. He determined he would quietly slip into the chamber and slash Siu Lung Lam's throat. Slowly, ever so slowly, he drew the stained curtain that covered the entrance. All three Triads were facing away from him facing the large window, which had been blacked out to obscure any curious spectators from the street below.

At the point in time, when Shyong Huei had fully slipped into the chamber, the wealthy addict looked at him at screamed. The ensuing blood-curdling scream from Shyong Huei standing in the doorway, fists clenched, blood now streaming onto the floor, caused all three Triads to simultaneously scream in fear. Blocking their exit of escape, Shyong Huei took a slow step towards the Triads; his face contorted, fiery eyes fixed upon Siu Lung Lam.

Siu Lung Lam, the consummate bully and by extension the consummate coward, instead of resisting Shyong Huei, sought to escape through the window and with a high-pitched falsetto squeal crashed through the opaque pane into the night.

The addict slumped back onto the table. Three thuds were heard in close succession as the Triads crashed into the street. Well known to the Kowloon community, the three men lay broken on the ground. Passers-by merely stepped over them if they were never there or never existed.

Shyong Huei had just become master of an opium den. He giggled childishly at the thought.

17. Unruhigen Traume

Do not go gentle into that good night,
Old age should burn and rave at close of day;
Rage against the dying of the light.

Though wise men at the end know dark is right,
Because their words had forked no lightning they
Do not go gentle into that good night

Dylan Thomas

Berenger met Singh VC with a big smile and a hearty handshake. Therefore, Berenger despite his saporous state had the presence of mind to realise that he was unconscious. His mind had returned to the German trench in Pozières. But his body lay with countless others wounded and desperately ill in a converted military hospital in England. He was oblivious to the storm howling outside.

Instead of pointing his rifle at Singh, they greeted like old friends. Berenger asked Singh about his wife and family. Surprisingly, Singh produced a family photograph; one which, he had previously omitted to produce upon their first meeting. He pointed out his doting mother, his proud father, his innocent loving wife and all his relations. Each received a warm epithet or a brief anecdote as to their character such that by the time Singh had finished, Berenger felt that he knew Singh's family intimately.

Berenger realised that not all members of Singh's family were spoken of as highly as his parents or his wife. But in the manner that Singh had spoken of them, Berenger understood that Singh had forgiven them for their trespasses. In recognising that he had trespassed against others himself, Singh hoped he would be forgiven.

Even the description of his wayward cousin, whom he caught stealing one of his goats before he left India for the war in Europe was couched in forgiveness and sentimentally. Singh noted a tear streamed down his cousin's face on the day he left for the train station to join the 39th Garwhal Rifles.

In the back of his cousin's mind, he knew brave Singh would probably not return. Embarrassed, he looked away so as not to reveal his sadness and shame, thereby depriving them both of a farewell glance. The episode of Singh's goat brought back pleasant memories and laughter. Singh said the attempted burglary was so bare-faced and amateurish that he could do nought else but laugh about it.

On that evening, Singh had told his father that he was going to serve India in the army. His father told him to put away such childish ideas and go to bed. Father told him he had responsibilities to his family and he was not going anywhere. Singh remained steadfast, standing in the same spot, not wanting to dishonour his father's desire for him to stay but quietly protesting by standing.

"Are you going to stand there all night?" father asked sarcastically.

"I will stand here until you permit me to join the Garwhal Rifles," was Singh's reply.

"You will be standing there for a long time then."
"I will be standing here a long time, father."
"You will die," said father, again sarcastically.
"I will die," said Singh resignedly.

A worried expression came over his father's face. Without moving as the sun sank into the horizon and the full moon rose into the sky bringing with her the wonderful spectacle of a warm Indian evening, Singh gazed into the stars and eternity.

Father retired to bed but he did not sleep. He lay awake looking at the moon for some hours, wondering and worrying about his son's stubborn stupidity. Eventually, he arose to check whether Singh had retired to bed but upon discovering him standing in the same place, legs quivering, he returned to his room more perturbed than ever. Finally, relenting to his son's desires, he fell asleep for the remaining hours of darkness.

The pain started in Singh's feet and crept up his legs spreading into his lower back. He was beginning to wonder whether he had made the right decision. He wondered if he could hold out until dawn.

Whilst imagining the vastness of space and trying to identify some of the constellations, Singh noticed silent, stealthy movement beneath the window from which he was looking. Although he did not immediately recognise the shape of the person attempting to quietly penetrate the goats' pen, the noises that emanated from the little herd rushing at him in the hope of being fed, when he opened the creaky gate, almost brought him tears of laughter.

Singh regaled his tale with such mirth that Berenger knew the aches and pains in Singh's back and legs had dissipated at least momentarily and permitted him to hold-on standing in the same position until the moon set and as always the sun's rays pierced the horizon.

Singh was laughing now as his cousin's hair-brained scheme had been thwarted by his lack of planning. His Cousin even tripped and fell on his face allowing the little goat to escape from his arms and run bleating back to his pen.

At that moment both Singh and Berenger let out a collective laugh and Berenger patted him heartily on his back, thanking him for such a fine anecdote.

It had brought to Berenger's mind the tale of a goat and his friend Wiremu Tamehana, the New Zealand soldier, who died at Gallipoli. But before Berenger apotheosised this young soldier as the best he had ever met, Berenger told Singh about the daring escape from prison during the Gallipoli campaign. Always downplaying his own part and highlighting the escapades of some small portion contributed by another escapee, Berenger had captured Singh's attention. Despite having no formal military training, Berenger referred to Avraham's plan to break out from Fort Kilitbahir in the Dardanelles as a calculated stroke of genius. Even the gormless Ali, who impulsively issued tirade of Turkish expletives at the Turkish guards, permitting their passage through the prison gates was retold as inspired stratagem.

Singh smiled, chuckled and nodded listening enthusiastically to Berenger's masterly ability to recount and embellish a tale. After Berenger had brought Singh to the point where the escapees had to cross No Man's Land, he paused dramatically.

Berenger's leadership had brought them this far. Without saying so, both Berenger and Singh knew that he had saved the lives of the escapees to this point. The dramatic pause precipitated an emotional epiphany to Berenger, which he had not previously considered.

Berenger had captured a nanny goat. Singh gasped in expectation; and Berenger had fed the remaining survivors with life-preserving goat's milk. Berenger had nearly died of dehydration and fatigue at this point. He had been hallucinating, talking to people, who were not there and was so severely dehydrated that he had lost track of time and sensibility.

Berenger suddenly realised that Wiremu had felt honour-bound to repay a debt. The debt accrued from the time Berenger and Wiremu met in Kilitbahir prison. Berenger had preserved Wiremu's life. Attempting to consider the situation from Wiremu's perspective was cathartic for Berenger.

Berenger believed there are moral duties in life. The reciprocation of an obligation merely reinforces the duty. Berenger's duty was to protect the lives of his men until he was unable to fulfil his duties; (or his men were no longer, his men). Although Berenger had not expected anything in return, it was naïve of him to think that the men would not believe they had a moral obligation to reciprocate.

The weight and worries of the world began to lift from Berenger's shoulders. He thought about Wiremu's selfless actions of standing up in No Mans' Land between the Turkish and New Zealand lines and thereby intentionally drawing the attention of Turkish sniper fire. Wiremu had allowed the remaining escapees to slither over the sandbags into the New Zealand trench to safety.

Wiremu knew he would be killed by being shot in the back by the Turks. He had calculated that the New Zealand sentries would recognise the Māori haka, and thereby refrain from firing at him in No Man's Land.

It then dawned on Berenger that Wiremu was repaying his debt not only to him but also to Kuehn and Ali; persons to whom, Wiremu believed he owed his life. *Utu* (reciprocation) was a construction of Wiremu's Māori culture and system of belief, not of Berenger's. Berenger did not believe he was owed anything. The repayment of the debt was for all three of the remaining escapees, not only for Berenger. Wiremu died consonant with his Māori warrior traditions, not Berenger's traditions. Wiremu was with his ancestors in Waikato, New Zealand now.

At this realisation, Berenger looked deeply into Singh's eyes, and although he tried not to, he broke down crying. Singh's resigned expression and kind eyes were salutary to Berenger, so much so that he closed his eyes momentarily. His heart and his conscience had weighed so heavily upon him this past year. Berenger felt a great cleansing of his soul. He felt his shoulders slump a little. He looked down at the ground where he expected to see the fine, dry, chalk dust of Pozières front but instead found lush green grass. The air tasted fresh, not foetid or cordite-filled, as he had expected.

Berenger wanted to continue his story with Singh but when he looked into the deep brown smiling eyes of the person seated next to him, Berenger found that they and the big smile which greeted him belonged to Wiremu.

Berenger wanted to embrace him but Wiremu brought him back to his senses.

"What the devil are you looking at?" Wiremu said sarcastically in Māori.

"What the devil have you done to your face?" Berenger greeted him laughing, but also in Māori: a language that Berenger did not realise he spoke.

The chiselled *tā moko* tattoo completely covering Wiremu's face denoting him as a fierce Māori warrior did not look so fierce to his friend Berenger. His handsome features, white teeth and the engaging smile remained distinctly Wiremu.

"*E tu* (Stand up)," said Wiremu.

As Berenger stood up he became more aware of his surroundings. Mist rose from the Waikato River as it meandered into the distance. Mixing with smoke from cooking fires, the sweet aroma of food wafted over from the far bank of the Waikato River. The laughter of little Māori children playing at the water's edge near the marae met Berenger's ears. The mellifluous tui began to cry out. Rich greens and earthy browns of many varieties struck Berenger's eyes. The life forms of the forest came together in their morning choir.

Wiremu faced Berenger, placed his strong hands behind Berenger's head.

"What the devil are you doing?" exclaimed Berenger. Expecting to be kissed, Berenger no longer desired to embrace his old friend.

After Wiremu's nose pressed against Berenger's nose in a traditional Māori hongi, Berenger in characteristic Australian brogue let out a tirade of expletives. This was met with an equally colourful tirade by Wiremu, laughing in response.

They stood on the bank of the Waikato River in silence watching the children splashing about in the water. Presently, an attractive young Māori woman displaying a *moko kauae* chin tattoo, came down to the river's edge to fill her calabash. She gazed momentarily from across the river and as if sensing Wiremu's presence smiled and diligently set about her work. Wiremu smiled back, somewhat coyly Berenger thought, for someone, who was supposed to be a fierce warrior and ostensibly no longer able to be seen by human eyes.

"So this is it, Wiremu?" Berenger eventually said.

"This is it, Berenger," Wiremu nodded.

"Heaven?" Berenger enquired.

"Heaven," Wiremu nodded.

Berenger extended his hand to Wiremu. Wiremu smiled. They shook hands in reconciliation.

"*Hāere rā, e taku hoa* (Goodbye, my friend)," said Wiremu. Before Berenger could respond all had disappeared.

Berenger lay supine, shallow-breathing on his bed. He had unconsciously thrown his blanket to the floor. An over-worked nurse had stopped to gently place the sheet and blanket over him and by not tucking them in, allowed Berenger some freedom of movement beneath. A concerned expression, followed by a damp cool cloth being passed gently across Berenger's forehead before she was required to rush off to attend to an endless supply of the sick, wounded and dying.

Berenger had survived the explosion in the South Australian trench at Pozières unlike Captain Hemple, who had been killed immediately; or Lance Corporal Albert Watts, who now lay in a hospital in France sans legs. But in the unsanitary conditions of the field hospital in France, Berenger had contracted what came to be described as the Spanish Flu. Consequently, he was in grave danger.

Berenger finally believed he had given his best for his country. He had resolved his internal conflict, which he had been carrying with him about the death of Wiremu Tamehana. For Berenger, Wiremu's absolution was enough for him to let go.

In his mind, he could see a light in the distance. Some friendly voices beckoned him. He approached the voices to find it was Breaker Morant. He was back in the dry heat of the South African war. Neither Breaker nor most of his section ever made it home to Australia. They all sat their horses, smiling down at him.

"Good to see you, mate," Breaker said.

"Good to see you," the rest of Breaker's troop chimed in.

There was one more horse than there were mounted riflemen.

"Berenger, it's about time you learned to ride, mate," Breaker said.

"We'll soon be flying, mate," sang Jack, one of the mounted rifles' men.

The others laughed. Berenger did not laugh. He still felt guilty had let his horse die on the journey to South Africa, mostly to spite his father. Breaker had not let him learn to ride and Berenger was required to run everywhere during his training. But Berenger had displayed empathy for one of the horses, emaciated and dehydrated, standing alone in his kraal. Although this was not much, he moved the horse to another stall so at least some small breeze could cool him.

It would have been an Elysian existence to return Berenger's troop. But the Elysian images began to flicker as literary characters remonstrating the indulgences of a wasted earthly existence began to replace them. The indecisive Ilya Ilich Oblomov laying in bed in his Persian gown, just about to roll out so that his pudgy feet could slip seamlessly into overly accommodating slippers. He sensed Raskolnikov's endless emotional turmoil after murdering the corrupt pawnbroker Alyona Ivanovna. Then the image of Oblomov appeared again. This time dying in bed: a completely wasted life unlived.

These images became juxtaposed with the struggles of Berenger's life. Struggles which, Berenger did not incline to return. Berenger knew he had to wake up. The stimulus, which had entered his mind had not motivated his nervous system to regain consciousness. In his dream, he threw himself on the ground to wake himself up but only succeeded in arousing the attention of friendly little Fuchsl, who thought he might lick Berenger's face and play a game.

"Go away, little Fuchsl," said Berenger in a more avuncular manner than Fuchsl's' previous owner. Fuchsl did not go away and kept jumping around Berenger, licking him on the face.

When Fuchsl's little tongue darted across Berenger's mouth, and Berenger caught a taste of little fox terrier slobber that was the last straw, and like Fuchsl's' angry previous owner, Berenger tried to slap deft little Fuchsl around the ears. Adroitly avoiding Berenger's flailing fist, Fuchsl jumped back on Berenger licking his face over and over.

Berenger had almost relinquished himself to this friendly little dog's ministrations covering his face with his arm. When he removed his arm, another image had taken its place. An image so insalubrious that Berenger could not but help stirring his body. Puck, a company commander's batman was bending over him again. His face was only inches from Berenger. And again Berenger could see a large drop of mucus precariously dangling from Puck's nose.

"Not again," Berenger audibly mumbled.

Thunder from outside echoed throughout the ward. The ward lights flickered. Lightning momentarily illuminated Berenger's face. The mucus drop in Berenger's dream became bigger and bigger and dangled ever more precariously, finally forming a string. This sword of Damocles ignited a spark in Berenger's mind triggering movement in his body. His hands turned into fists as he was about to clobber Puck. The drop entered squarely into Berenger's open mouth just as Berenger was trying to tell Puck to, "Piss Off!"

Berenger immediately opened his eyes. Staring back at him from above were the tearful eyes of his wife Juliana; tears streaming down her face. Berenger's fever had broken. Innately regaining composure as a panacea for embarrassment and for want of something to say, Berenger, blurted out in an affected English accent, "Oh, it's you."

Juliana, desperately tired and relieved, against the military hospital's Standing Orders lay her head down upon Berenger's chest.

The End